THE
ANTIQUARIAN

THE ANTIQUARIAN

Matthew Baca

Sunstone
Press

SANTA FE

Sunstone books may be purchased for educational, business, or sales promotional use.
For information please write: Special Markets Department, Sunstone Press,
P.O. Box 2321, Santa Fe, New Mexico 87504-2321.

Book and cover design ▪ Vicki Ahl
Body typeface ▪ WTC Our Bodoni
Printed on acid-free paper

Library of Congress Cataloging-in-Publication Data

Baca, Matthew, 1959-
     The antiquarian / by Matthew Baca.
          p. cm.
     ISBN 978-0-86534-729-8 (softcover : alk. paper)
     1. Tewa Indians--Fiction. 2. Time travel--Fiction. 3. Religious tolerance--Fiction.
     4. New Mexico--Fiction. I. Title.
     PS3602.A232A79 2009
     813'.6--dc22
                                        2009029989

WWW.SUNSTONEPRESS.COM
SUNSTONE PRESS / POST OFFICE BOX 2321 / SANTA FE, NM 87504-2321 /USA
(505) 988-4418 / ORDERS ONLY (800) 243-5644 / FAX (505) 988-1025

**Dedicated to San Lorenzo,
Patron Saint of Librarians**

CONTENTS

Preface

This book is a work of fiction derived from a real incident of cultural and religious tolerance that ultimately led to the peaceful coexistence of two very different peoples. The goal of this publication is to convey that lesson while providing an entertaining story for the reader.

The Pueblo ceremonies I have depicted are based on the writings of Tewa author and anthropologist Alfonso Ortiz in his book *The Tewa World: Space, Time, Being and Becoming in a Pueblo Society*. Mr. Ortiz's writings are not without controversy, and I apologize in advance to those who take exception to his work.

—Matthew Baca
2009

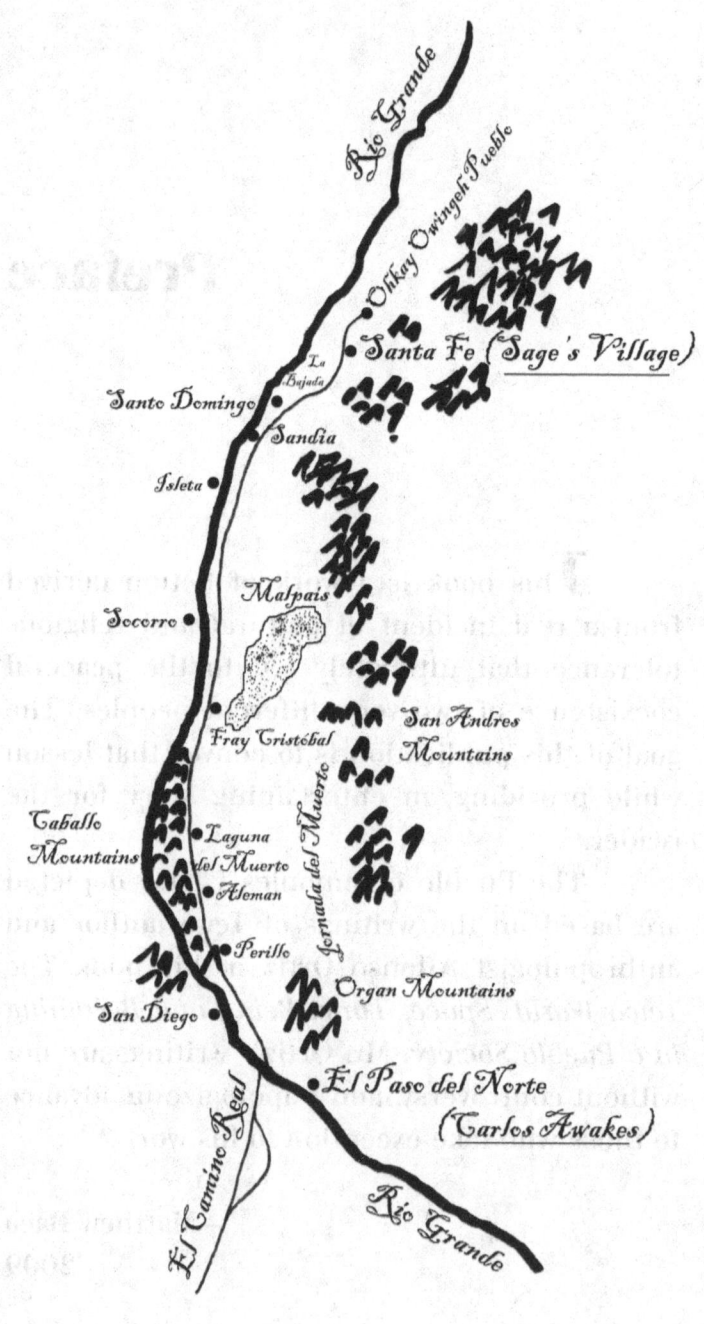

Rio Grande

Ohkay Owingeh Pueblo

Santa Fe (Sage's Village)

La Bajada

Santo Domingo

Sandia

Isleta

Malpais

Socorro

San Andres Mountains

Fray Cristóbal

Caballo Mountains

Laguna del Muerto

Aleman

Jornada del Muerto

Perillo

Organ Mountains

San Diego

El Camino Real

El Paso del Norte (Carlos Awakes)

Rio Grande

1

A New Job

"**O**kay, how about this one?" On the card was a painting of a can of Campbell's New England Clam Chowder.

"Easy. *Campbell's Soup*. Andy Warhol. Pop Art."

"Good, and this one," she said, her tiny brown hand flashing a card with a picture of a bronze sculpture of a man and woman kissing.

"Almost as easy. *The Kiss*, Auguste Rodin, Post Impressionist."

"All right," she said, shuffling through the stack of cards piled on the kitchen table. "Let's see you get this one."

"Ummm. *The Persistence of Memory*, Salvador Dali, Surrealist. Looks like the clocks are made of melting wax, doesn't it?"

"Looks more like melted cheese to me, but

you got it. How about this one?" she asked, holding up a card with a painting of a woman hanging laundry while a young girl watched.

"Give me a second. *Woman Hanging up the Washing.*"

"That's kind of obvious."

"It's Impressionist," I said, ignoring her comment. The artist's name was right on the tip of my tongue. I leaned back in my chair and stared up at the ceiling. No help there. I pulled gently at the tiny hoop earring clasped to my earlobe for a moment. Getting my ear pierced during the summer with the help of a couple of my friends had caused quite a commotion around the trailer, especially since we had used one of her sewing needles. Better not to remind her of that.

"Is it...Claude Monet?"

"Nope, Camille Pissarro."

"Damn!"

"Carlos!"

"Dang! I meant to say dang, Mom."

"I know what you meant to say. Let's just watch the language, especially around your sister."

"It's no big deal, Mama. I have heard those words before, "Sage said, lying on her stomach with chin propped in her hands in front of the TV in the family room. The volume was down low, but since the family room, kitchen and dining area are all really one room in the front part of our trailer, it is pretty hard not to hear the noise from the TV when it is on.

"They say a lot worse than that on TV," she continued. "On this show I'm watching the father is always calling his son a dumb ass."

"Sage!"

"But that's what he calls him."

"I don't care what he calls him. Fourteen-year-old girls, and seventeen-year-old gentleman for that matter," she said, shooting a look over at me, "don't use that kind of language. But enough of that. C'mon, Carlos, let's go through the pictures again."

"No time now, Mom. Carlotta is expecting me at noon," I said, getting up from my chair. "Besides, I'm tired of looking at all these old pictures. This class is a waste."

"Art is not a waste and I wish you would quit saying that," she said, "and the answer is still no. You're not dropping art to take shop."

Mom knew taking art really bugged me. We had gone round and round since school started a month ago. During my junior year I had taken first year shop, which turned out to be pretty lame. Mostly it was things I already knew how to do. In seniors' shop we would be making real stuff like furniture and cabinets. I had hoped that if I kept the pressure up she would finally give in. I mean, who wouldn't rather be working with wood and drills and saws and lathes instead of looking at a bunch of paintings by a bunch of people who'd been dead practically forever? Well, at least most of them. Warhol's not been dead that long. But she had stuck to her guns and so far I'd had no luck, and I didn't figure I would now.

"Mom, I've taken just about every class you wanted me to. I didn't complain when you made me drop family studies for second year algebra or weight lifting for world literature. And both of those were Advance Placement classes."

"And because they are AP classes you'll be able to get credit for them when you get to college," she said.

"I know, and I'm not complaining. The thing is, I like working with my hands. I want to build things."

"Carlos, I am not saying you can't build all the houses or office buildings you want when you get older. I just want more for you than working with a hammer and a screwdriver."

"I guess I don't see anything wrong with working with a hammer and a screwdriver," I said sharply, "and I don't see why you do. That's the way dad made his living before he died, you know."

Now I knew I had gone too far. Sage stared over at me with an angry little frown on her forehead. Mom just looked down at the flash cards in her hand. She takes after her mother, who was from the Ohkay Owingeh Pueblo thirty miles north of us. Like a lot of Pueblo Indians, Mom is a pretty small lady, and as those words had come out of my mouth she seemed even smaller.

I went around the table and put my hand on her shoulder.

"I'm sorry, Mama. I didn't mean to say that." She tilted her head back and looked up at me. I felt like I was towering over her. Most of my genes seemed to have come from my dad, who was much taller than most of his Spanish cousins walking around our hometown of Santa Fe.

"It's all right, *mi chavalito*," she said, patting the hand I had placed on her shoulder. "I know you like working with your hands, Carlos, and you're good at it, just like your daddy was. But I also know how hard it was for daddy. He was always going from job to job looking for someone who needed a good framer. Since you were babies we wanted more than that for both you and Sage. If you want to be a builder, that's great. Only you will be the one in charge. Instead of working as a framer like daddy, you'll be the one who supervises the framers, and the electricians and plumbers. With a good education you have a much better chance of giving orders, instead of being ordered around."

"I know that, and I am going to go to college. I just don't see how art is going to help me in the real world," I said, shaking my head from side to side.

"You don't know what you are going to find in the real world, Carlos. None of us do. For all you know, you might be sitting in a bank someday trying to get a loan to build a hotel or office park. The bank president is sitting with you talking about the project and trying to decide whether to take a risk on you. He has looked at your plans, and weighed your experience, but is still undecided about what to do. Then you notice a painting hanging in his office and you say 'Oh, I love Monet, he and Pissarro are my two favorite impressionist artists.' All of a sudden the bank president looks at you differently. He looks at you with respect, impressed by your knowledge. And maybe that is what it takes to help him make his decision. The next thing you know you have your financing."

Leave it to Mom to come up with the way my art class might influence a bank president some years off in the future. The thing is, she is usually right. Most people who meet her, or see her, hardly give her any notice. At least that's what she says. She thinks it's because she is short and dark, and usually quiet around people she doesn't know very well. But really, she is as sharp as they come. If I'm having a hard time with one of my math problems, she'll read an example in the book and within a few minutes figure out the answer to whatever I'm working on. Sometimes I think she spends more time reading our literature books than either Sage or I do. One of the things she most regretted, she said, was that she had never even thought about going to college back when she was in high school. It just wasn't something women did.

"Okay, I give in," I said, bending over and kissing the top of her head. "I'll stick with the class. I'd sure hate to lose the chance to be a builder because I don't know the difference between the Impressionists."

She laughed and everything was okay again, but then, as usual, only for a moment. "C'mon, Sage, Carlos is going to drop his flyers for Carlotta and we need to get you some soccer shoes."

Sage jumped up and shut off the TV. Her frown had disappeared, replaced by a big smile and dark brown eyes shining with happy anticipation. Unlike me, she takes after Mom's side of the family.

"Big Five is having a sale on their shoes. Brand new Adidas are only thirty dollars," she said.

A pained look came to Mom's face. But then, with a cheery note in her voice, she said, "All I have is ten dollars, Ms. Sage, so I guess we'll be shopping at Goodwill today. I saw a nice pair of shoes on Thursday that looked like they had hardly been worn. I would have bought them but I want you to try them on first."

The smile on Sage's face and the shine in her eyes disappeared.

"Mommy, you said when I got to high school I would finally get to wear a new pair," Sage said with an accusing tone that sounded just like the one Mom used when the garbage hadn't been tossed or the floor hadn't been swept. I didn't say anything. Instead I looked down at the table, pretending to study one of the cards lying there. Not that it mattered. I figured that in about two seconds my coffee can money would be in play.

"I know, Sage. And I'm sorry, but that's all I have and I don't get paid until Thursday."

And on Thursday, I thought to myself, that money will have already been spent because the trailer park rent is due on Wednesday.

Yup, the coffee can was definitely in play, big-time.

"How about using your credit card?" Sage asked, a tinge of hope in her voice.

"It maxed out when I replaced the fuel pump on the car."

Tears welled up in Sage's eyes and Mom looked like she was going to cry as well. I gave a small sigh and surrendered again.

"How much do you have left from taking care of Duke and Apollo?" I asked Sage. Duke and Apollo are the neighbors' poodles. Sage had fed and walked them for two weeks while their owners were out of town.

"Eight dollars and forty-two cents. I had ten but I needed some hair ties."

"I think there's fifteen dollars in the coffee can. With that and Mom's ten dollars you have over thirty dollars."

"I don't want to use your money for the soccer shoes, Carlos," Mom said. "If we don't stop using that money you'll never be able to afford a motorcycle." She hesitated for a moment and then continued, embarrassed. "Anyway, there is only ten there. I had to put five dollars worth of gas in the car."

Carlotta paid me for dropping flyers and I'd been hoping to buy a beat up off-road motorbike that could be made street legal. So far it had turned out to be a lost cause. Pretty much we survived on Mom's paycheck from the diner and a little social security money we'd get every month because of Dad dying. And when those ran out there was no place else to turn but the coffee can. Actually, I was surprised there was even ten dollars. Usually by this time of the month it was empty.

"It's not a problem, Mom. Anyway, the longer into winter I wait, the cheaper they'll be. Nobody likes to ride in the cold." I turned to Sage, feeling a little irritated but trying not to show it. "Hurry up, Sage, I need to get going. I don't want Carlotta getting mad at me. She hardly ever notices me, but for some reason she wanted me to be at the café today at twelve o'clock on the dot." Sage gave me a grateful look, which I chose to ignore, and headed to the bedroom she shared with Mom in the back of the trailer.

"Thank you, Carlos. You made your sister very happy. And you know you make me proud," Mom said. "I'll try and put the money back in a couple of weeks."

"Whenever you can, Mom. Now I really have to run or I'll be late."

I thought of our money problems as I rode my bicycle over to the café. I seemed to be thinking about that all the time lately. Though I'm not too crazy about spending my money on Sage, it doesn't really bother me that much. When Dad was really sick toward the end—when he knew he wasn't going to beat the cancer—I'd sat with him one day while he lay on the pullout couch in the family room that doubled as my bedroom. Though that was five years ago, it was as clear today as it was then. He'd told me, between his bouts of coughing, that when he wasn't around anymore I'd be the man of the house. He'd told me that I would be responsible for taking care of Mom and Sage. It was a heck of a responsibility and a heck of a lot more important than a crapped-out motorbike.

Nope, it wasn't spending money out of the coffee can that bothered me, but more the way something always seemed to be blocking me when it came to earning more money for the can. When Dad died I was only twelve years old, much too young to do anything but cut lawns and pull weeds during the summer. For a real job I had to be sixteen. Then when I turned sixteen I found that most places didn't want to hire a kid who could only work part-time after school or on weekends. When I turned seventeen last spring, I figured I'd at least be able to finally get a full-time summer job. Unfortunately, my timing was horrible. Gasoline prices were shooting through the roof, which, with a recession pounding the country, slowed the number of tourists coming to Santa Fe. The restaurants weren't even hiring dishwashers. Mom tried to get me a job at the diner by the interstate where she waits tables. She said the owner, Henry, wanted to help, but business was so slow he was doing both the cooking and the dish washing. As cheap as Henry is, he'd probably have waited on the tables too, if he could have figured out how to pull it off.

I'd found out that finding a job wasn't easy, and looking for one was hard work.

The closest I had come to steady work was dropping flyers for *Carlotta's Café del Sueños and Sweet Treats. Sueños* means dreams in English, which I guess is where she comes up with a lot of the crazy and delicious dishes she serves. During the week Carlotta runs daily specials on what she calls her Eclectic Traditional New Mexican Cuisine, and every Saturday I'd take a load of flyers describing the upcoming specials and distribute them to all the homes and businesses in the area. I was paid a dime for each one I dropped. On a good day I could make over twenty dollars.

I rolled into Carlotta's, glancing at my watch as I climbed off my bike. High noon. Right on time.

I chained my bike to the leg of a wrought iron bench in front of a pink Buddha fountain that greeted the café's customers in the outside courtyard. I liked the Buddha. He always had the same big smile on his face, as if he was glad to see me. Entering the café I spotted Carlotta's daughter, Madalena, and waved. She was busy with a customer at the cash register, so I waited patiently, listening to Tibetan music chanting at me from hidden speakers and studying the latest painting hanging on the wall behind the counter.

In the center of the canvas was a circle showing a nighttime sky with distant twinkling stars. The dark edges of the sky turned to lighter blue as you looked toward the center, almost as though looking through a tunnel into the sky. Bordering the circle was an intricate ribbon with four evenly spaced stones. From a school field trip, I knew one was an arrowhead and I thought a flatter rock near the bottom center had been chiseled into a kind of knife used by the ancient Indians of northwest New Mexico to skin animals. I didn't know what the other two stones were.

"Hey, Carlos, *cómo está?* You like the latest?" Madalena asked, when she finished with the customer. Like a lot of Santa Fe's native Hispanics, Madalena's sentences are often a mix of both languages.

"Yeah, I do, especially the ribbon."

"That's a Celtic ribbon, pronounced with a kay as in keltic. If two people love each other, it's suppose to link their hearts over time and distance. At least that's what it said on one of the websites I checked. The ribbons have been around for thousands of years."

I don't know where Carlotta and Madalena find all the things they have decorating their place, but it is always interesting.

"So, you here to pick up the flyers?" Madalena asked.

"Yup. How many do you have today?"

"Three hundred. Mama had me print an extra hundred. She's making seafood tostadas, *calabacitas* and apricot pecan pie on Tuesday and grilled portabella mushroom tacos, Spanish rice and apple almond tarts on Thursday. Think you can deliver them all?" Madalena asked, reaching beneath the counter and pulling out a plastic grocery bag packed with bright purple flyers.

Three hundred, I thought, that's going to take a while, but that means an extra ten dollars. "No problem, whatever I don't finish today I'll drop tomorrow. How's your mom doing anyway?"

"Her? *Ella está bien.* We should all be so healthy. Next month she turns ninety and we're going to have a big birthday party for her. You gotta make sure and come."

"Ninety!" I exclaimed. "Why Madalena, that means she must have had you when she was over sixty years old!"

Madalena blushed lightly beneath her olive skin, and her eyes sparkled. "What a charmer you are, Carlos. You must have the *señoritas* falling at your feet. I will turn fifty-five next Spring. Not looking to bad for a *viejita*, eh?" Madalena was actually quite pretty. There were a couple of shiny gray strands peeking through her thick black hair, and a few lines around her eyes, but not many.

I smiled. "No, Madalena, not bad at all. I'll bet you have all the *señores* falling at your feet."

Madalena blushed again and laughed. "Enough of this

chit-chat. Carlotta wants to talk with you before you leave."

Well, that explained why she wanted me here at noon sharp. But I wondered what she wanted to talk about. Carlotta hardly ever spoke to anyone that I could tell. Sometimes, on the rare occasions when she happened to be in the dining area, I'd say hello. Most of the time she'd give me a curt nod of her head and wish me good day in Spanish. Other times she seemed to look right through me. I figured it was because she was so old, and maybe a little senile.

"Where is she?" I asked.

"At the table in the corner," Madalena said, pointing. The table was mostly hidden behind some kind of frond tree in a huge terra-cotta pot.

"Who's with her?" I asked, noticing another person through the breaks in the leaves.

"*Quién sabes,* a friend from many years back, I think. I've seen him visit her before, but she doesn't say much about him."

Taking the bag of flyers from Madalena in my left hand, I walked toward Carlotta's table. As I came closer I heard the murmur of the man's voice followed by the smooth laughter of a young woman. Funny that Madalena hadn't mentioned a third person. I peaked around the frond and realized that it was Carlotta, with her back toward me, who was laughing. And just as the laughter hadn't sounded like her scratchy old voice, neither did she look like herself from behind. Her hair was shinier and fuller, and her shoulders—long stooped from age—were pulled back as she sat straight in her chair.

As I quickly stepped up to the table, Carlotta was still laughing softly and dabbing with a tissue at a tear in the corner of her eye. The deep lines on her dark thin face were hardly noticeable and the hollowness in her cheeks had disappeared. I've seen Sage and Mom spend hours giving each other makeovers, but I had never seen a transformation like Carlotta's. And it was done so well you could hardly tell she was wearing any make-up at all.

Across from Carlotta was an elderly man wearing a gray suit with a white shirt and black tie. He was not as old as Carlotta, I decided, probably about fifteen or twenty years younger. Though most of his hair had gone to gray and was quite thin on top, he still had a bit of the original brown showing through. He also sat very straight in his chair, but his feet just barely reached the floor. I guessed he was probably just a little over five feet tall. For someone who looked to be in his mid-seventies, he seemed to be in pretty good shape. On the table in front of them were two white teacups with a matching pot, and a small plate of *bizcochito* cookies.

His attention was focused on Carlotta and he was smiling pleasantly at some joke they had shared. Then he turned to me.

I felt my whole body shudder as our eyes locked. For a brief moment the penetrating stare of the man's bright blue eyes was like a pile driver smacking into the back of my brain. Then the look softened and he nodded slightly with a look of satisfaction on his face.

"Carlos," Carlotta said. I looked over to Carlotta... and Carlotta was Carlotta again. The flat gray hair, stooped shoulders, deep wrinkles and hollow cheeks of the ninety-year old woman were back. I stared at her in surprise, wondering if my imagination was playing some kind of trick. But she didn't seem to notice and continued as if nothing had happened.

"I would like for you to meet *un buen amigo que*

también fue mi maestro, Doctor Antonio Lopez."

I have to admit that I'm pretty good sometimes. Even though my brain was totally overloaded, I managed to extend my hand with hardly a tremor, and return the doctor's firm handshake. While we exchanged the usual 'please to meet you' type greetings, another part of my brain was trying to figure out whether I had correctly interpreted what Carlotta had just said.

Both my parents spoke Spanish as their first language. In fact, my family on both sides, like most natives of Santa Fe, had roots that extended back to the Spanish Conquistadors. Mom also spoke a little *Tewa*, which, along with some Spanish, was the language of her pueblo. The thing is, they had intentionally never taught Sage or me how to speak anything but English. This went back to several bad experiences they had as young children when the school teachers made life hard for any student speaking Spanish. They didn't want the same thing to happen to us, so English it was. Most of the Spanish I had picked up as a kid came from the conversations Mom and Dad had had between themselves, which were usually conversations they didn't want Sage or me to hear. But even so, I was pretty sure that Carlotta had just told me that Doctor Lopez was not only a good friend but had at one time been her teacher. The only thing I could figure is that maybe he had taught her to cook or something. He sure couldn't have taught her in regular school, unless he was a lot older than he looked. If he had taught Carlotta in school, he'd have to be over a hundred, at least. Although, from what I thought I had just seen, my sense of age perception was probably open to discussion.

"*Sientase*, Carlos," Carlotta said, pointing a bony finger to the chair between them. "You are in need of work, *que no?*"

I nodded and gratefully took the offered seat. I was feeling weak in the knees.

"Well, Doctor Lopez is in need of a worker. So I thought, you know, that maybe the two of you should meet. Maybe work out some kind of arrangement."

The weakness in my knees disappeared, replaced instead by a small churning in my stomach and a sudden case of clammy hands. I felt like I had been called to the front of the class to do a problem on the board with everybody watching. Only this was no algebra problem in front of my friends; this was a big-time opportunity to finally get some money into the house. I only wished I'd known earlier why Carlotta wanted to talk with me. At least then I could have worn something other than a shirt with patches on the elbows and last year's pants riding two inches too high above a pair of dirty sneakers.

"And an arrangement may be in the offing, Carlotta, but first we must see if this young man possesses the skills required for the more arduous tasks," Doctor Lopez said. The words rolled off his tongue smoothly with just a hint of an accent. "Carlos," he said, "do you know what an antiquarian is?"

I thought I might, but decided a wrong answer was risky. I shook my head.

"I'm an antiquarian, Carlos. I collect antiques and antiquities. These are old and sometimes quite valuable objects that appeared during times that have long since passed. They may be as small as a thimble or as large as a marble sarcophagus. Some are as light as a cobweb, while others are as heavy as the tusk of a woolly mammoth. They come from the dawn of man and from the ends of the world."

I didn't quite understand everything the Doctor had said and remained silent, watching as he paused for a moment

25

to take a bite from one of the cookies, followed with a sip of tea.

"I have been an antiquarian for a very, very long time," he continued. "So long that many of the items now coming through my door have seen fewer years than I." Carlotta made a small noise that might have been a stifled giggle. Doctor Lopez paused long enough to look over to her and smile. I'm not sure, but I think he also winked.

"It is a beautiful collection, Carlos," he continued, "and I fear I am not providing the care that is necessary if I wish to keep it in the best possible condition. It also seems the physical aspects of my business have become more strenuous than they were in my younger years. For these reasons—and others—I have decided to hire an assistant to help me in my work. Would you be interested, Carlos?"

I was proud of myself. When I answered my voice was steady, "I don't think you will find anybody more interested in this job than me."

"Very good," the Doctor said, "Tell me about yourself."

What could I tell him that would land me this job? I wracked my brain for a couple of seconds. There didn't seem to be a whole lot to tell.

"Well, I'm a senior over at Santa Fe High School, and after I graduate next summer I'm hoping to go to college. I like to read and play sports, and I live at home with my sister and mom." He continued to look at me expectantly. "Uhhh...I'm taking honors math and English, art, computer networking and political science." There was an uncomfortable silence, but I didn't know what else to add to my painfully thin resume. Carlotta delicately dipped her cookie into her tea before taking a small bite. She didn't seem to be paying attention to us.

"No history classes?" he finally asked.

"Oh, yeah, world history."

Again, an uncomfortable silence. I stared down at the tablecloth trying to figure what else I could say. Carlotta continued to nibble and Doctor Lopez took another sip of tea. My stomach grew tighter and my hands clammier. I was really messing up the interview. The doctor put his cup down on the saucer.

"So, you're taking an art class?" I nodded. "What type of art do you like best?"

Which did I like best? They were all pretty much the same to me. But I knew that wasn't the right answer.

"The Impressionists," I said, thinking of Mom's bank loan scenario.

"Oh? That was a good era. Are you more a Pissarro or Monet fan?"

"Uhhh...I guess Monet."

"Really. I'm more partial to Pissarro, but art is a matter of taste." For a second I thought he and Mom had set this up as a joke. He even seemed to have a small smile tugging at the corners of his mouth.

"Do you make good grades in school?" he asked, changing the subject.

"I'm carrying a three point nine grade average," I said with some pride in my voice. I'd worked hard for that average, especially since I was taking AP classes.

"Hmmm...that is good. Will you be able to work and keep your grades up?"

"Yes, sir," I said. "Mom says that barring the Second Coming, Sage and I are going to college. Case closed."

He nodded in agreement. "Make sure you listen to her.

Can you work after school and on Saturdays?"

"Yes, sir."

"Are you strong in the back?"

"Do you mean can I lift a lot?"

"Yes. And more." Doctor Lopez leaned forward over his cup and his voice became a whisper. "Can you ignore your muscles when they are screaming at you to stop whatever you're doing? Can you keep moving forward when your body wants no more than to lie down and go no further, or when hunger or thirst are so strong that you can think of nothing else?"

My eyes widened and I looked over at Carlotta. She had snagged another *bizcochito* and was nibbling at it like a mouse nibbles on a piece of cheese. She still did not seem to be paying any attention to our conversation.

"I can keep on going," I answered, trying to make my voice sound strong.

Doctor Lopez paused for a moment and I again felt the full force of piercing blue eyes. But this time the penetrating stare seemed to spread throughout my entire body.

"Are you stout in spirit?" he asked, a deadly serious expression on his face.

I hesitated before answering, looking him straight in the eye and trying to figure out what he was asking.

"I'm not exactly sure what you mean by stout spirit, Doctor Lopez. But if that's what you need, then that is what I will have."

The doctor smiled. "It is not what I need, Carlos" he said very softly. "It is what you will need."

I returned his smile with a wary smile of my own. He seemed not to notice. Reaching into his shirt pocket, he pulled out a small card and handed it to me.

"Here is my address. Do you think you can find my home?"

"Number One, *Animales del Picacho*," I read out loud. "Is that somewhere by *Camino Picacho*? I ride my bicycle down that street sometimes."

The Doctor nodded. "It is off *Camino Pichacho* where it dead ends."

"I don't think I've ever ridden up that far, but I'm sure I can find it."

"Good. Now for compensation, will ten dollars an hour be adequate?" the doctor asked casually.

I felt my eyes open wide and my voice cracked a little when I answered. "More than adequate, sir."

"Then be at my house promptly after school on Monday."

And that was the end of our meeting. Afterward, the doctor gave Carlotta a big hug and, speaking to her in Spanish, promised to come back for the portabella tacos. He shook my hand and wished me good-bye as we left the café together and then, with a light and quick step, he disappeared into the crowd of Saturday shoppers.

I managed to drop all the flyers that afternoon, moving fast so I could get home and tell Mom and Sage my exciting news. When I told them Sage squealed with joy—new soccer shoes and a job in one day—but Mom seemed a little quiet. I thought she might be worried about me working for some strange man I had met in the café, but that wasn't it. In fact she thought she had read about him in the newspapers. No, she wasn't worried, she said, she was sad. Her baby was becoming a man.

School ended early on Monday because of teachers In Service, which is a faculty meeting where the teachers all gather to discuss things going on around the school. Or maybe it was to celebrate one of the teacher's birthday. Either way, I didn't have to rush around trying to find Doctor Lopez's house. I was a little worried about that. I'd looked at the street map in the telephone book and found where *Camino Picacho* came to an end up toward the foothills east of town. But the map didn't show a street named *Animales del Picacho*. I thought about buying a regular street map, but at four dollars a pop I decided to rely on the directions the doctor had given me.

So I rode my bike up *Camino Picacho*, which made a slow steady climb toward the Sangre de Cristo Mountains. At first the homes on the street were bunched tightly together, most of them at least a hundred years old. After a while, as I pedaled up into parts of the street I had never ridden before, the homes became bigger and much more spread out. Most of the yards were landscaped in southwestern style with piñon and juniper trees and native gramma and buffalo grass. About a mile further I saw where the road came to an end and *Animales del Picacho* began its ascent up a low round hill.

As I began the climb up the lane, the excitement I had felt since meeting Doctor Lopez grew stronger. I'd often read books where the characters get so excited they can barely contain themselves, but never really knew what that meant. Now I knew what the authors were trying to convey. It seemed as if high charged electricity was running through my body. All my senses were attuned to the beauty of the world around me.

Then the landscape changed. Tall trees lined the road on either side. Behind the trees stood a wall barely low enough for me to look over from my bicycle seat. On the other side was a growth of oddly shaped bushes.

A gentle breeze, warmed by the bright autumn sun,

blew softly against my face. High above me the changing leaves clung to their branches, crowding together in a great red and gold ceiling. The leaves seemed to have captured the rays of the sun, only to release them in dazzling displays of color. For a moment I felt as if I was flying through an immense kaleidoscope, the whirling shimmering leaves having become millions of bright and beautiful jewels. It felt great to be alive.

Up ahead, at the end of the lane, I spotted a break in the wall where the tunnel of trees converged in a cul-de-sac. As I got closer I saw the entrance to a long curved driveway that led from the curb to Doctor Lopez's home. At least I thought it was a home. If so, it had to be the biggest house I had ever seen. Over the years Santa Fe's character has attracted many of Hollywood's top movie stars and New York type corporate executives. You can see their mansions scattered in different upscale developments around town. But those I'd seen were dwarfed by the one in front of me.

I let my bicycle coast to a stop at the driveway entrance and spent a few minutes examining the house and yard. The house was set back from the street on the crown of the hill. The exterior walls were dark brown stone. Each stone was roughly the size of a dishwasher. Tall rectangular windows with half moon arches were evenly spaced along the wall facing the street. Red clay tiles capped the sloped roof of the house. Beneath an open portal supported by marble columns was a giant wooden door resting on massive black iron hinges.

Along the walls and throughout the garden were dozens of bushes. The taller ones reached the eaves of the house, while others were no bigger than a child's balloon. Each bush was unique—some were broad leafed, some thin leafed, and others had pine-like needles. The colors of the leaves ranged

31

from ruby red to an iridescent violet.

I realized now why the bushes I had glimpsed briefly through the trees and over the wall had seemed to have a familiar shape. Each and every bush was trimmed into the form of an animal. Giraffes grazed alongside lounging gazelles, and apes reached for low hanging tree branches. Rabbits crouched next to howling wolves, and miniature bulls and horses romped around the tree trunk legs of a herd of elephants.

It was like nothing I had ever seen. Anyone passing would have probably thought I looked like a radar antenna atop a battleship, my head swiveling back and forth as I tried to take in the scene in front of me. Only there was no one to see me, and around me it was eerily quiet.

I spent a moment listening to the silence. There were no car or jet noises, no barking dogs or shouting children. The breeze had died down and the leaves were no longer rustling. I spotted some birds perched on one of the bushes. They watched me intently, but made no effort to fly away.

I climbed off my bike and pushed it up the drive. Though the grade wasn't particularly steep, I ran short of breath and a light sweat broke out on my back by the time I reached the porch.

Not wanting to disturb the silence, I gently placed my bicycle against one of the marble columns and moved slowly toward the front door. It had an iron knocker cast into the shape of an old-fashioned square lantern. I took a deep breath, lifted the knocker and brought it down three times. A few moments later the door swung silently open.

2

The Great Room

"Ah, Carlos," the Doctor said, looking very small in the frame of the immense door. "Right on time. Please come in."

I thought it might be rude not to comment on his strange bushes, plus I was downright curious. "This is a pretty nice zoo you have here. You should be included on the Santa Fe Chili Pepper Tour." The Chili Pepper gives tourists open-air tours in busses painted to look like chilis. "They all look so real. Did you trim them yourself?"

"Yes, this is one of my hobbies; turning living bushes into living art. Maybe sometime you'll be here to see them under the light of a full moon with just a whisper of fog. That is when they really seem to come alive.

"Enough about the animals. Come inside

and let's see if we can get you working." The doctor stood aside as I stepped up onto the porch and crossed the threshold into a short hall paneled in light yellow marble. At the end of the hall was a closed pair of shiny brass doors, and to my left, through a partially opened wooden door, I could see a stainless steel exhaust hood over a black countertop covered with books, beakers and flasks. Across from the door, hanging against the wall like a giant flag, was a richly embroidered tapestry with the image of a great tree. On one side of the tree the blue water of a sea stretched to the horizon. Swimming in the water were stubby-legged lizard-looking creatures. On the other side was a lush green garden. Near the base of the tree, at the water's edge, a man and woman stood side-by-side. The man's arm was lovingly draped across her back, while her head rested lightly against his shoulder. Above them, a dense canopy of branches grew out from the thick trunk. Delicately woven within the leaves were hundreds of people that seemed to be from many different races and cultures.

"That is my office and laboratory," Doctor Lopez said, easily pushing the heavy front door closed with one hand while pointing to the partially open door with the other. "No need to go in there now. Most of your work will be done in the Great Room and the antechambers."

I followed Doctor Lopez as he walked to the brass doors at the end of the hall and pulled them open. The light from the hall spilled across the threshold into the unlit room, illuminating a medieval suit of armor that stood just on the inside of the doorway. For a second I got the feeling that someone or something was staring out at us from behind its louvered visor. Beyond the suit of armor the room was cloaked in complete darkness.

"I know it's here somewhere," Doctor Lopez said, stepping into the room, his small hand sliding up and down along the wall in search of a light switch.

"Ah ha, I found it," he said, and the next moment the room was flooded with bright white light. "Welcome to the Great Room, Carlos."

My jaw dropped open and I heard myself gasp.

Spread out across an immense room was a collection of art, artifacts and goods that would have made any museum curator envious.

The Great Room's name barely did it justice: it was in fact a magnificent work of architecture. The ceiling had fifteen elegantly curved concave sections that lay three abreast across the width of the room and in rows of five along its length. At their lowest point, where the corners of the sections met, solid black marble columns rose from the floor to the ceiling. Hanging from the center of each section was a crystal chandelier.

The knight I had seen in the shadows was only one of about twenty lining the wall at the top of the room. The metal gauntlets they wore on their right hand grasped the hilt of half-drawn swords, while their other hand held tightly to wooden spears with wicked looking iron tips. They were like sentinels standing guard over the king's treasury.

In front of the knights were ancient manuscripts, beautifully bound Bibles and white marble busts wearing crowns of gold. Hanging on the walls and perched on easels scattered throughout the room was a magnificent assortment of paintings in gilded frames. Glass cases held finely crafted ornaments made of precious metals, wood, and bone. From primitive stone knives and hammers to delicately sculpted statues and intricate stained-glass windows, the variety seemed endless. Through three arched doorways in the opposite wall the collection continued into other rooms. I figured these were the antechambers Doctor Lopez had spoken of out in the entry hall.

"You can take a breath now, Carlos," Doctor Lopez said.

I hadn't realized I was holding my breath and slowly let it out. "This is…is…awesome, Doctor," I said, stammering to find the right words to describe his collection.

"Awesome? Yes, I suppose it is. This is the collection I told you about. I have spent my life collecting and studying what you see before you."

I turned my gaze from the room to the doctor. I could only think of one response.

"Why?"

The doctor's expression turned thoughtful for a second and then he gave a small chuckle. "A very good question, Carlos, but a question to which there is not a simple answer. I guess the easiest answer is I study to learn, and by learning, I will understand."

"Understand what?" I asked, hoping I wouldn't irritate him with my curiosity.

He looked at me keenly. "As much as is humanly possible." He took a moment to gather his thoughts. "You see, Carlos," Doctor Lopez continued, "I want to understand how a newborn calf, less than an hour into the world, is able to stand for the first time and go straight to the milk waiting in the udder between its mother's back legs. I want to know how big the universe is and how small it once was. I want to know…."

He paused and brought up his right hand until it was a few inches in front of his face. Slowly his little finger began moving rhythmically as if to some unheard music. Then the other fingers started moving, first together as if he was waving, and then apart as if he was striking the keys on a piano. Then they stopped and the fingers came together making a tight fist. He relaxed and dropped his hand to his side while taking a deep breath. This he held for a few seconds and then let it out slowly. Suddenly he laughed a great booming laugh that echoed throughout the Great Room, causing me to start.

"I want to understand," he continued, "why my body can do that." Doctor Lopez was silent for a moment. "But most of all, more than anything else, more than math and chemistry and astronomy and geology and biology, I want to understand what we are and why we do the things we do."

I followed Doctor Lopez as he walked out into the room.

"I've found some answers but many elude me. I know our world today is the sum total of our past. And in both the past as well as today, I study the beauty human nature has created and," he said in a slightly weary tone, "the darkness of evil that so often rears its appalling head."

I felt a small chill, almost as if a cold draft of air had blown across us. Suddenly it seemed that the Great Room wasn't quite as bright as it had been a moment earlier.

"I am an antiquarian. The things spread out across this room are antiquities. In the antechambers are other parts of my collection. I study civilization as if it were a tree: a tree of many branches, but born of one seed. And though some of the branches may have withered and died, and those that continue to grow have changed and taken different shapes with the passing of each season, the seed that gave life to the tree remains the same."

He suddenly stopped walking and turned to me. We were standing next to a glass-enclosed pedestal. Underneath the glass was what looked like half a human jawbone with only a few teeth still intact.

"There are many experts who believe the seed of the human tree took root in Central Africa about two million years ago. Of course that was long before any records were kept, so much of what is known comes from studying the evidence that was left behind. From this evidence, we know the seed sprouted, and the branches formed. Over the centuries, the human race multiplied and migrated around the globe. Though very similar to modern man in many ways, these first people were physically smaller and their brains were not as large or complex as they are today. It was only about forty-five thousand years ago that we evolved into what we are today. Do you know how old the Earth is, Carlos?" he asked.

"Four billion years is what comes to mind, but I'm not sure where I got that number."

"Well, wherever you got it, it was from a good source. Most scientists think that is the approximate age of our world. Now consider that man has been here in his present physical shape for only forty-five thousand years. Compare that to four billion years."

I considered the relative size of the two numbers and the number of zeroes involved—45,000 years vs. 4,000,000,000 years. Take away three zeroes from each side to simplify: 45 years vs. 4,000,000 years. The sheer size of the numbers was still bigger than I could really grasp, so I tried to think of some examples that would give me a good comparison. What I came up with was surprising to me. It would be like a shovel full of dirt tossed on a mountain, a thimble of water taken from a lake, or my day's pay from Carlotta resting beside a four million-dollar fortune.

"Talk about new kids on the block," I said, whistling softly through my teeth. "We've hardly been here at all, compared to what has passed. It kind of makes me feel insignificant, if you want to know the truth."

"Quite right, Carlos, we are, as you say, the new kids on the block. But it is not my intent to make you, or me, feel insignificant. I believe we need to look at the world around us as the product of over four billion years of work. How can we be insignificant if the product of those billions of years is a species that can contemplate existence, and death? We are only insignificant if we do not meet the responsibility we have been challenged with, which is the challenge of improving and bettering that which has come before. To fulfill our responsibility we must use the gifts that have been given to us, whether through evolution or by our creator, and comprehend what we examine. So let us meet our responsibility and try to understand.

"It is of great significance to my work, Carlos, that modern man is relatively new, and, as we know him, physically the same today as he was ten and twenty thousand years ago. Let us return for a moment to my analogy of the tree. For the sake of this discussion, let us assume it is an oak tree. During the spring months, the tree produces a new set of leaves that fall off and die when winter sets in. The cycle repeats itself every year. Old leaves die and new ones are born. They are not the same leaves, but they are all oak leaves, and they all have the same traits and characteristics of the leaves that came before them.

"The tree of man is no different," he continued, "and that is a key factor in my work. Stone Age man made his tools from rocks because he did not know how to forge and use metal. The people of the Iron Age didn't know that adding tin to iron would make a new metal called brass. And that is no different from men in the nineteenth century not knowing about the operation of an automobile—"

"Or," I interrupted grinning, "people not knowing fifty years ago how to play video games."

"Touché, Carlos," Doctor Lopez said smiling. "So we know men and women were no less intelligent ten thousand years ago than they are today. Our intelligence is a common thread. But that intelligence is only one of many threads. Archaeologists have unearthed evidence that shows the most ancient tribes fed and took care of those unable to care for themselves. Now we have charities and social programs that perform the same functions in our present day world. There is no difference; compassion, like intelligence, is but another thread.

"Unfortunately, the threads are not always so benevolent. The threads of envy, brutality, and greed are as much with us today as they were with our earliest ancestors. And, interestingly, none of these traits are confined to any single branch or part of the tree. Man shares these characteristics across the face of the world. But that is hardly surprising. As I said, we are all of the same seed."

As he spoke, Doctor Lopez's voice had taken on a somber note. He was silent for a moment, then he looked around the Great Room.

"This is my work, Carlos. Through these things from the past I study the common characteristics of humanity. From the time people were banding together and learning the use of fire to the modern day of space travel, super computers and weapons of mass destruction, I try to find answers to the question of why we are as we are."

I did not reply, but stood looking at the doctor's face. What a strange little man I had come to work for. But something in the way the doctor spoke, or in the things he said, gave me a sense of anticipation.

I think my job had found me.

"Come now," the Doctor said, "it has been a long while since I have walked through my collection, and it will do us both some good."

For the next three hours, we meandered through the Great Room. The doctor spoke almost nonstop as we moved from one exhibit to another. Sometimes he would pause to pick up an item and study it as if for the first time. Other times he would make me laugh with a funny story related to his acquisition of a particular object.

The antechambers, though much smaller than the Great Room, housed a considerable number of exhibits. They ranged from the recurved tusk of a woolly mammoth (the doctor hadn't been kidding in Carlotta's café, but he had failed to mentioned the elaborate carvings in the ivory) to small displays of concrete from the Berlin Wall and the World Trade Center.

The sun was setting and there was a chill in the air when Doctor Lopez escorted me back onto the front porch.

"Thank you for coming, Carlos," the Doctor said. "I think you will have the opportunity to learn quite a bit while working here."

"Thanks for taking a chance on me," I said. "I'll do my best to make sure I don't let you down."

"Your best is all I ask for, Carlos."

I rode my bicycle down the drive and into the street.

Looking back over my shoulder, I saw Doctor Lopez standing next to a lion-shaped bush. He seemed to be talking to himself. Maybe singing to the twilight. It was, after all, a beautiful evening deserving of song.

I started humming as I pedaled down the lane and headed home.

When I returned the following day, I found Doctor Lopez waiting at the front door with a bottle of furniture oil in one hand and a dust rag in the other. He led me through the Great Room and into one of the antechambers, where I spent the remainder of the afternoon cleaning and oiling 17th century French furniture. A small card of heavy paper was attached to each piece of furniture with a strong thread. On the card was a brief description of the object, including the origin and time from which it came. Occasionally there was a paragraph describing significant events related to the piece. Doctor Lopez encouraged me to read the cards as I worked.

The rest of the week proceeded in a similar manner. After school let out, I would hurry over to Doctor Lopez's and receive my assignments for the day. Generally they involved some type of cleaning and polishing, or the moving of an exhibit from one place to another. After the doctor had assigned me my afternoon tasks, he would usually disappear into his office until the end of the day. Every once in a while I would catch a glimpse of him across the Great Room or as he entered one of the antechambers.

Sometimes I thought back to my first meeting with the doctor, and his ominous queries about being strong in back and in spirit. So far the hardest jobs he had given me had done little more than cause a light sweat to break out on my forehead. I sure hadn't had any assignments like the kind suggested during our interview.

But as the weeks passed and autumn moved toward winter, I thought about his curious words less and less, and soon forgot about them altogether.

3

A November Storm

I finished washing the last of the mashed potatoes and turkey stuffing from the serving plate and passed it to Sage to be rinsed.

"You didn't get it clean. There is still some gravy on the edge," she said, shoving it back at me.

"Just rinse it off," I said, ignoring the plate in her hand.

"The key word is rinse, Carlos. I rinse, you wash. You didn't wash. See." She held the plate about three inches in front of my nose.

"Aaargh! You are a real pain, you know that?" I took the plate, gave the speck of gravy a swipe with the cloth and handed it back.

"Much better," she said, inspecting the edge where the offending spot had been.

Sage moved the plate from side to side

under the faucet stream and then set it on a pile of clean dishes that had held our Thanksgiving meal a short time earlier. I stuck my hands into the water beneath the suds and searched for any spoons or knives I might have missed. Finding none, I pulled the plug. While the water was draining, I peered through the small window over the sink. The rain had stopped for the moment and the rays of a weak afternoon sun had broken through the clouds. It's too wet to go outside now, I thought glumly to myself, and even if doesn't rain again, it was too late in the day for the sun to dry much of anything.

Mom was getting ready to work the swing shift at the diner. Sage and I would be on our own until late in the evening. That meant either watching the tail end of holiday football games on the small black and white television or playing another game of cards, neither of which seemed particularly appealing at the moment.

"Don't forget to put out the trash tonight, Carlos," Mom said, as she put the finishing touches on her lipstick in front of the small mirror glued to the door of the refrigerator. "Make sure you wrap the turkey bones in a plastic bag or we'll have every cat in the neighborhood digging through our garbage."

"Don't worry, I will."

"And there's a load of clean laundry in the basket. Can you guys fold it and put it away before you go to bed?"

"No problema," I said. At least that would kill about fifteen minutes worth of a six hour evening. Now what to do for the other five hours and forty-five minutes?

"Thanks, Carlos," she said, capping the lipstick and dropping it into the front pocket of her white waitress uniform that reminded me of something a nurse would wear. She stepped over between the two of us in front of the sink and put her arms across our shoulders. "I'm sorry I have to work today but I'm off on Sunday. Maybe we can go to a movie or something."

Before either of us could reply, the phone on the small kitchen counter let out a shrill ring. Mom stared at the instrument as if it was an unpredictable animal that might bite her. She let it ring a second time, and then probably decided that even a collection agency wouldn't be calling on Thanksgiving. She scooped up the receiver and pressed it to her ear.

"Hello. Oh, hello, Doctor Lopez," she said, looking over at me with a questioning look. She listened for a moment and then spoke. "I look forward to meeting you someday also, and it is no interruption at all. We've already finished our dinner." For some reason I felt my stomach jump. I took a step closer so I could hear what was being said on the other end of the line, but all I heard was a faint crackling noise.

"Yes, we had quite a downpour about an hour ago—a lot of thunder and lightening. It felt like it was going to blow the trailer over." Some more crackling sounds came through. "Uh-huh, uh-huh. Oh no, that's awful."

"What? What's awful?" I whispered urgently. Mom shut me up with an outstretched hand.

"I wish Carlos could help, Doctor, but I'm just about to leave for work and I can't leave Sage here by herself." She stopped talking and listened. "Uh-huh. Are you sure that would be okay? I won't be able to pick them up until late tonight. Will that be okay also?" She nodded her head as the voice on the other end spoke. "Let me ask them."

Mom put her hand across the receiver and spoke to us in a whisper. "It's Doctor Lopez. He has a leak in his roof and the rain has flooded one of the rooms in his house. He wants to know if the two of you can come over and help him clean it up."

I looked over at Sage. She wore a big smile and her eyes looked at me in a conspiratorial manner. I felt a surge of excitement and we both nodded our heads in unison. Mom hesitated for a moment, then turned back to the phone.

"I guess it will be okay. I'll drop them off on my way to work. We should be there in about fifteen minutes. Why don't you give me your phone number in case we are delayed." She smiled at something the doctor said and wrote his number on a scrap of paper. "Uh-huh, no, no problem. It will keep them occupied while I'm at work. Okay. We'll see you in a few minutes. Good-bye."

She placed the receiver back on the phone and gave us an 'I'm not too sure about this' look, but whatever concern she had she kept to herself.

"All right, you heard what I told him. Finish rinsing out the sink and grab your coats. We have to get going right now if I'm going to drop you off at Doctor Lopez's and make it to work on time."

Two minutes later we pulled away from the curb in front of the trailer and headed toward Doctor Lopez's house. Mom turned the wipers on just long enough for the blade to make a few swipes across the windshield and clear the raindrops that still clung to the glass.

"I hope this is the last we see of this rain for a while. I sure don't want to be driving home in one of those downpours at eleven o'clock tonight."

I didn't want to be driving home in the rain either. The thunderstorms that had swept into town the day before were unusual in how fast and how hard they hit. Usually, by this time of the year, rain would come in low gray clouds that hung heavy over the city for a day or two, dropping their moisture in a slow steady drizzle that would sometimes turn to a heavy wet snow. But these storms had rolled in over the mountains east of town and migrated across the sky in fast-moving black waves, unleashing their fury in torrential rains and violent bolts of lightning that streaked across the sky before slamming into the ground. Then, with the force of the storm spent, the clouds would retreat back to the mountains and hang there ominously as they built strength for the next onslaught.

Mom turned onto *Animales del Picacho*. All the leaves had fallen from the trees lining the road and their bare branches reflected a grayish color as the sun sank in the west. As we approached the front drive leading up to Doctor Lopez's home, I thought about the afternoons I'd spent working for the doctor. I had told Mom and Sage about his strange home. Mom had said something about him probably being a bit eccentric, while Sage had shown an immense curiosity about my job. As soon as I came home from work, she would immediately pepper me with questions about my time spent at Doctor Lopez's. Sometimes I got a little tired of her hanging all over me, but I tried to be patient and describe the various nooks and crannies of the house, and the wondrous objects there.

"What in the world...? Is that Doctor Lopez on the ladder?" Mom asked, bringing the car to a stop at the top of the drive.

"I'm pretty sure that's him," I said. Doctor Lopez, wearing a knee-length, bright green rubber slicker and black rubber boots, was perched halfway up a long ladder that rose from the ground to a gutter running along the eave of the house. The ladder was placed just to the side of one of the huge front windows. An all-season hedge—a holly I thought—with shiny green leaves ran the length of the wall and was trimmed to the same height as the windowsill. However, directly in front of the window, the hedge had been allowed to grow upward so that it could be seen through the glass from inside the house. It was on this section of the hedge that Doctor Lopez was busy at work with a large set of pruning shears. From where we sat in the car, the fast-moving blades of the shears appeared as a blur. Snippets of brush and a fine mist rising from the raindrops on the leaves surrounded the doctor. The portion of hedge in front of the window was taking the shape of a large bird with outstretched wings. He was so engrossed in his work that he didn't seem to notice our arrival.

"Yup, that's Doctor Lopez, Mom," I said.

"You know, wearing that green raincoat, he looks kind of like a giant gummy bear," Sage said from the back seat. I started to reply with a sharp retort, but didn't. She was right, he did look like a giant gummy bear.

"I wonder why he's out here doing yard work instead of cleaning up his mess," Mom said, peering intently through the car window. Then she turned to me. "Well, tell him I'm sorry I can't meet him right now. I'm already going to be late for work as it is. You kids scoot now, and I'll see you at a little after eleven."

We hurried out of the car and watched as Mom carefully backed down the drive. We turned to Doctor Lopez and found him looking down at us from his perch.

"I'll be right down," he shouted. "Two snips and I'm finished." He studied the bush for a moment, snipped once, looked at it again, and made a final cut. With surprising agility he climbed down and walked over to where we stood by the front porch.

"Greetings, Carlos," he said cheerily, "and greetings

also to you, Sage. It is a pleasure to make your acquaintance."
Sage, whose attention was focused on the animal topiary
surrounding us, turned to the small man as he spoke.

"Pleased to meet you," she said in a shy voice and
reached out to shake the hand that was offered to her. A
sudden gust of wind blew across us and Sage shivered.

"Let's get out of the cold," the doctor said. "I know a
nice cup of hot chocolate would certainly seem in order, but
that must wait until we have attended to our work in the Great
Room. Buckets and mops are at the ready, and we need to put
them to good use before the next thunderstorm arrives. Time
is of the essence now, so hurry along."

"If time is of the essence, why is he out here trimming
his hedge?" Sage whispered as we followed Doctor Lopez up
onto the porch. I shushed her and shrugged my shoulders.
The Doctor's unusual behavior had sparked a small feeling of
expectancy. Something felt different, but I told myself it was
nothing other than arriving at his place at a time when I was
usually leaving. For some reason my reassurances didn't feel
very convincing.

Doctor Lopez led us through the front door, past the
Tree of Life tapestry and down the hallway into the Great
Room. Sage's eyes opened wide and it was her turn to make
like a radar on a battleship as her head swiveled back and
forth taking in the enormity of the room. The doctor gave her
a quick glance, but didn't pause as he walked quickly to an
area by one of the windows. I followed behind, grabbing Sage's
hand and dragging her along.

Heavy purple velvet curtains were drawn across the
window. A small but steady trickle of water flowed from a
crack in the ceiling above the curtains, feeding a small pond

of water that had formed on the floor. I could see that several smaller pieces of the collection had been moved out of harms way. All that remained was a glass covered exhibit table that rose from the center of the puddle like an offshore drilling rig anchored at sea. Two mops stuck straight out from a blue plastic bucket next to the table.

"I don't think the water has gotten behind the curtains, but I'd better open them to see," Doctor Lopez said, reaching for a soft thin rope dangling from the rod supporting the heavy cloth. He pulled at the rope and the curtains separated, revealing one of the large windows that looked out onto the front yard. Still holding Sage's hand, I felt her shudder. Staring through the window was the bird the doctor had been shaping when we first drove up. All the red berries on the holly bush had been removed except in the middle of the face, giving the sculpture a crimson-eyed stare that seemed to focus directly on us. Two leafless branch stubs gave the appearance of a formidable looking beak.

"How do you like my owl?" Doctor Lopez asked. "She's the newest member of my horticultural menagerie."

"She looks very real," I said.

"She looks really scary," Sage said, stepping up to the window for a closer look.

"Good," said the doctor with a note of satisfaction in his voice. "Then my work has had the desired effect. I'd hate to have thought I spent the afternoon trying to create a fearsome owl that instead looks like a hungry pigeon."

I couldn't shake the feeling that the giant bird was watching our every move. But it wasn't in a menacing sort of way. It was as if it were a family pet watching the comings and goings of its owner's friends.

"Why do you want a scary owl?" Sage asked slowly, her eyes fixed on the bird with a mesmerizing stare.

"Eh? Well...hmmm, I guess you never know when a scary owl will come in handy."

"Handy for what?"

"Why, handy for any situation where a scary owl could be of use." Sage gave the doctor a puzzled look and started to ask another question. Before she could, the doctor cut her off and continued speaking. "But that is enough of the owl for right now. We need to move this table before it becomes water damaged." The doctor stepped out into the puddle and grasped one end of the table. "I'll take this side, you take the other, Carlos. Let's see if the two of us can move it out of the water so you and Sage can mop up this mess."

I stepped cautiously through the water to the table.

When we had finished, Sage stepped over and peered at the artifacts that had been carefully arranged beneath the glass. On one side was a display of several crosses. Some were made of wood, others of copper and silver. One looked to be of solid gold. On the other side of the display, lying next to the crosses, were several masks shaped and painted with different expressions. Much of the paint had faded and peeled away, but the differences were pretty striking. Most had huge grins and funny noses, but several had narrow squinting eyes with thick gruesome lips. There were small feathers or dried reeds tied with strips of cracked leather to some of the masks.

"Oooh, Carlos, look at all the funny masks." Sage leaned over the table until her nose almost touched the glass. "Are these old toys, Doctor Lopez?"

"Those? No, mostly they are masks that were at one time used in religious ceremonies."

Sage looked at the doctor with an exaggerated frown, as if she thought he might be pulling her leg. "I've gone to church almost every week since I was a little girl," she said, "and I've never seen anything like these."

"They weren't made for Christian services, Sage. They were used by the Pueblo Indians in their religious ceremonies." Sage continued to look at the Doctor with a doubtful expression on her face. "Each of the masks represent a spirit the Indians prayed to," continued Doctor Lopez. "Their priests would wear them and imitate the spirit during the ceremony. The religions of the Pueblos are hundreds, maybe even thousands, of years old, but masks such as these are still used today."

"Oh," Sage said in an uncertain voice. "Then how come you keep the crosses on the same table? Christians don't have those beliefs."

"I keep them together as one exhibit because they tell a story of tolerance, and the peace that often comes with tolerance. This exhibit is part of a story of the melding of two very different and distinct cultures."

"And what's the story?" I asked quickly. My heart was beating hard and an eerie feeling crept over me. Something was happening. I could feel it, but couldn't pinpoint it. It reminded me of a dream I sometimes have where I am reading a book. The letters and the words are all there, but I am unable to make sense of the sentences.

"It is much too long a story to be told now. You both have a lot of work ahead of you this evening, so I think we best save it for another time."

"Can you just tell us what it's about?" I persisted, "Not the whole story, but just a...you know..."

"A thumbnail sketch," Doctor Lopez said, finishing

my sentence. "Okay, but I'll have to make it a little fingernail sketch instead. Do you know when the first Europeans explored the Southwest?"

"They first came around fifteen forty, but then left and didn't return to stay until fifteen ninety-eight," I said, which is what I had learned in one of my history classes.

"That's right, the Spanish settled what they called New Spain, which we now call New Mexico, over twenty years before the Pilgrims landed at Plymouth Rock. With their soldiers came the friars of the Catholic Church. The friars took a dim view of the Pueblo religions and, as was their mission, began the conversion of the Pueblo people to Catholicism. Unfortunately, their methods became more and more severe as time went on and the Indians were intent on keeping their traditional ways. The soldiers, with the backing of the friars, systematically destroyed the *kivas* where the Pueblo people practiced their religion and they arrested the Pueblo priests. They hanged several of the priests and the rest they whipped and imprisoned."

"I thought you said this story was about religious tolerance," Sage said with a horrified look on her face.

"Hold on, hold on, I'm coming to that. The strong-arm tactics, which began when the Spanish arrived in fifteen ninety-eight, worsened and continued for a little over eighty years, until finally the Pueblos reached their breaking point and staged a revolt. Over four hundred settlers were killed and the Spaniards were driven out of Santa Fe and New Mexico back into old Mexico. Spain, as one of the most powerful countries in the world, could not allow open rebellion in its empire. A soldier by the name of Don Diego de Vargas was appointed governor, and sent back to Santa Fe to reconquer the Pueblos. Fortunately, unlike past governors, de Vargas realized real peace could only be won if the Pueblos were given their freedom, which included the right to practice their native religions. He brought this message to the Pueblos, and, for some reason, they took de Vargas at his word. The Spaniards were allowed back into Santa Fe in the year sixteen ninety-two without any blood being shed. From that day on the foundation for a peaceful coexistence had been laid. It was not the end of the horrible violence perpetrated on the Indians by the Spaniards, but the beginnings of peace through tolerance had arrived."

The sun had now set and darkness fell outside the window of the Great Room. In the distance the sky briefly lit up as lightening flashed in the clouds above the mountains. The room was silent except for the drops of water falling from the ceiling to the floor. Doctor Lopez stared up at the crack.

"It doesn't seem that leak is going to stop unless we can drain some of the water that has collected up there. I think a gutter clogged with leaves is partly to blame for this mess."

"You're not going to try and clean the gutter in the dark, are you?" I asked. My concern was only partially for the doctor. I really didn't want him to leave us alone in the room by ourselves.

"It shouldn't be too difficult. The ladder is already set next to the gutter. I'll only have to climb up and scoop out whatever is blocking the drain. I meant to do that when I was up there earlier, but I got side-tracked trimming the owl. I'll be back in a minute or two. In the meantime, you two can mop up down here."

The doctor buttoned up his slicker and walked across

the Great Room. Sage and I looked at each other and then picked up the mops and began swabbing at the water.

We had almost filled the bucket when a bright flash of lightning, followed almost instantaneously by a crash of thunder, lit up the yard outside the window. The crystal chandeliers flickered twice and then went out completely. A loud, windy howl filled the darkened room. Outside the window a bolt of lightening cast an electric blue light through the pelting rain pouring from the sky.

In the blue light, through the rain streaked window, we saw a terrifying sight. Doctor Lopez's ladder had fallen almost on its side, lying at an awkward angle against the hedge, while the doctor clung with both hands to the edge of the roof. He was kicking his legs frantically in search of a foothold.

"Carlos!" Sage screamed.

But I was already moving to the window. My fingers fumbled at the latch trying to make it open. It was a simple slide bar, but many years of nonuse had sealed it shut. I bent my fingers around the clasp holding the bar in place and gripped it tightly, pulling with all my strength. Then the clasp came loose abruptly and the rushing wind blew the windows violently inward, throwing me across the wet floor and whipping the heavy curtains into an undulating frenzy. In an instant I was back on my feet and at the window. Doctor Lopez was invisible in the darkness, but I could just see the end of the ladder resting against the hedge. I leaned out of the window as far as I dared and stretched my hand to the ladder. A few more inches and I would have it—if only I didn't lose my balance and topple out over the windowsill. Behind me I felt Sage grab the back of my belt and try to anchor me as I leaned out even further. The owl's wet leaves, mixed with the stinging rain, slapped at my face. My feet were starting to slip out from underneath me when the electric arc of another lightning bolt hit directly in front of the window. I felt the heat of the strike, while the blast of thunder knocked Sage and me off our feet and sent us rolling into the room and crashing against the table. Rushing wind like a screaming animal surrounded us. I started crawling back toward the window, not wanting to stand for fear of being thrown back across the floor. But the fury of the wind had destroyed the curtains, ripping their anchors from the wall and blowing them across the room where they landed on top of us.

I blinked my eyes, but couldn't see anything except the afterimage of the lightning bolt that was now branded onto my retina. I wasn't sure if the roaring sound in my ears was from the storm or the concussion of the thunder. The pressing weight of the wet curtains was suffocating me and I tried desperately to push the cloth from my face. I might as well have been at the bottom of a deep pool trying to push the water away. My hands met little resistance but the curtains continued to press in on me. I tried scrambling across the floor on my stomach, but only felt myself getting more entangled in the cloth.

I heard Sage calling out to me. I yelled back and tried to move toward where her voice seemed to come from. But my struggle was useless; the curtains were like a snake that had its prey in its coils.

A moment later I lost consciousness.

4

Carlos Awakes

A low hum was all I could hear, but I could breathe again. The darkness, and the curtains, had disappeared and bright morning sunlight filled a room I had never seen before.

"*Hay, muchacho.* What a dream you must have had. You have your bed sheets wrapped around you like the husk on an ear of corn. Let me help you from this cocoon."

The Great Room, and Sage, were gone. Instead, a light-skinned young woman with a dusting of freckles across her nose smiled down at me. Her blue eyes held a look of concern.

Since that first moment I had seen Doctor Lopez trimming the owl, I had felt something strange taking place around me. Now I didn't know where I was or what had happened. Maybe the lightning and thunder had damaged some part of my brain, or maybe I was just having a bizarre dream. Whatever it was, I didn't like it.

"You must hurry and eat. The meeting will be starting in less than an hour and you are to stand as Governor de Vargas' attendant. You should be very flattered; he asked for you personally. But don't let that go to your head," she cautioned, giving me an affectionate cuff above my ear. "He will send you away in a moment if you give any indication that you are unable to carry out your assignments."

There was a gaiety to her voice and she spoke so rapidly that the words seemed to flow over each other. Though she spoke in Spanish, I understood her completely. I sat up in bed, untangling the sheets and considering what she had said. Governor de Vargas had to be Don Diego de Vargas, the man who led the reconquest of Santa Fe. And if that was so, then I was dreaming, or hallucinating, about a time over three hundred years in the past. I let this crazy thought run through my mind as I swung my feet over the edge of the bed. For a second I thought of throwing myself back onto the mattress and pulling a pillow over my head. Instead, I stood up—a little wobbly—and took in the surroundings.

The room was smaller than the bedroom in the trailer back home. The narrow bed pressed up against a kind of cock-eyed mud wall half covered with cracked gray plaster. It looked as if a good gust of wind could bring the whole thing down, if it didn't fall under its own weight before then. On the opposite wall a crucifix hung above a washing basin resting on a small table made of rough-cut wood.

"I had Ramirez clean your boots," the girl said. "There will be many important people at this meeting and you should

59

look your best. Judging from your appearance, you have a ways to go.

"You should see your hair," she continued with a giggle. "It looks like an untended haystack. That will never do. Dunk your head in the basin and wash the *lagañas* from your eyes, while I brush the dust off your clothes."

She reached behind the open door and retrieved a shirt and pants from a hook embedded in the wall. With a swift movement, she pushed the bed sheets to one side and lay the clothes out flat, brushing at them with the tips of her fingers. I opened my mouth to say something, but nothing came out. I didn't know what to say. Or, I had a hundred different things to say and didn't know where to start. I decided it was best, for the moment, to believe everything around me was part of a whack-on-the-head induced hallucination. So I walked, self-consciously, over to the basin on the little table.

The woman looked to be about eighteen or nineteen years old, and was very pretty. I wasn't at all comfortable moving about in nothing but what resembled a pair of boxer shorts. But she didn't seem to notice anything out of the ordinary, and continued to brush at dusty spots on my shirt while softly humming to herself.

The basin was fairly large and I was able to dunk my head completely. I closed my eyes as I went under and the sound of the humming disappeared when my ears went below the water. The world around me disappeared in the same way it disappears for an ostrich when he sticks his head in the sand. Unlike the ostrich, I was pretty sure that whatever lurked above was still there. Okay, Carlos, just relax and watch the events unfold.

Easier said than done.

In addition to the mass confusion spinning through my brain was the worry of what Sage might be going through back in the Great Room—if she was still there. I pictured her at the window fighting the storm and trying to help Doctor Lopez. Then it occurred to me that she might also have been tossed back to this seventeenth century dream with me. If that was the case, then where was she? She's back at Doctor Lopez's, I answered myself. Remember, this isn't real.

Suddenly, I felt a very real sharp pinch on my bottom and my head shot up out of the basin. I spun around with water dripping from my hair onto my shoulders and chest. "Hey, what the heck?" I sputtered, trying to wipe the water from my eyes with the back of my hand.

"What are you doing there? You think you are a fish or something? I thought maybe you had drowned standing up," the young woman said, eyeing me curiously.

I grabbed a corner of the sheet from the bed and used it as a makeshift towel to dry my hair. "I was just trying to wake up. You didn't have to pinch me, *Señorita*."

"Oooh, *Señorita*, he calls me. My, how formal we are today, or is this to be the new style of the governor's attendant? Now that you are standing with such important men as those who surround the governor, you will no doubt distance yourself from your friends with charming formality," she said. Her lips formed an exaggerated pout, but there was a smile in her eyes. "I will no longer be Sofía—baby-sitter when you were young and now your friend—but instead, *Señorita*, your acquaintance." She clasped her hands to her chest and looked down in a dejected manner. "Alas, if that should come to pass, life will have lost all meaning." She held the pose for another second and then let out a peal of laughter. "You silly goose, get dressed. Your breakfast is probably cold by now."

I used my fingers as a makeshift comb and dressed quickly. The clothes were the right size and the boots fit perfectly. I then followed Sofía through the doorway into a small sitting room built as badly as the bedroom. The whole place had a slap together feel that reminded me of houses one and two in the story of *The Three Pigs*. An outside door opened into a plaza surrounded on three sides by adobe huts similar to the one I had been in. A much larger and better built structure dominated the remaining side of the plaza.

The people milling about could have come from either a Hollywood film stage or a living museum. The few women I saw were wearing long dresses and cloth bonnets that protected them from the glaring sun. The men outnumbered the women. Most of them were standing about in knee-high boots and vests made of leather.

"Look at all the soldiers," Sofía said. "They are waiting to hear what the governor says in the meeting. Come on, Ramirez is waiting for us."

I followed her through a narrow deserted alley that ran alongside the large building and opened to a small courtyard in the back. She led me to a chair at a wooden table set beneath a scrawny shade tree.

"Ramirez, we're here," Sofía shouted in the direction of a doorway opening into the courtyard. "And, I know at least one of us is very hungry."

Nothing happened for a few seconds, other than a few unmistakable kitchen noises coming from the shadows beyond the door. Then a short brown man dressed in a white shirt and trousers resembling burlap pajamas came out. His age was hard to guess—probably somewhere between his mid-fifties to his late eighties. A huge stomach hung over the cords holding his pants in place and his rolling double chin hid any sign of a neck. The hair on top of his head had long since disappeared, but the long gray strands sticking out from his cheeks and jowls seemed to make up for what he lacked. He carried a wooden tray that held two plates loaded with scrambled eggs and thick slabs of steaming ham. Beside them stood a small bowl filled with slices of brown-skinned fruit with pink melon flesh. It didn't look particularly appetizing to me, but when Sofía saw the fruit she jumped from her chair, rushed over to the man and kissed him noisily on his hairy cheek.

"Ramirez, where in the world did you get the mameys?" she asked. "You know how much I love them."

"*El gobernador* have mameys brought for meeting. I not think there nothing bad if some come to your breakfast," he said, pleased by Sofía's reaction. He spoke slowly—as if he had to search in his head for each word. And the words carried a strange and heavy accent.

"You must join us, Ramirez."

"Oh, no. I have much preparations still."

"Join us just for a moment," she persisted. "You can tell us what is happening. I have no desire for ham and eggs when there is mamey at the table. I'm sure you don't want to see this good food go to waste."

"It be sin to feed to dogs," he said, convincing himself. "I sit with you."

We took our seats. The eggs needed salt, but the ham was tender and moist. The mamey seemed a bit overripe, but tasted sweet. Ramirez did not need any further encouragement once he had made up his mind to join us. He dug into the food and emptied his plate before I had eaten half my eggs.

With a contented sigh—and a worried look on his face—he leaned back into his chair. Sofía held the mamey in her hand, nibbling on a small piece, and studied Ramirez carefully. Ramirez's mood had distracted her.

"You worry yourself needlessly, Ramirez. No more harm will come to your people," she said. She looked over at me. "You know his mother is of a southern Indian tribe that no longer fights us."

No, I didn't know that, I thought to myself. How could I know that? I've never seen this man before and I have no idea who or what his people are. But I didn't say anything.

Ramirez gave Sofía a long thoughtful look before speaking.

"No, they not fight. They not fight with wooden clubs against soldiers carrying sharp swords and long spears. But northern Pueblos have many men. They have swords and spears. They fight and many men die. My father come from Spanish and my mother from Indian. So I come from both. No matter who die, I mourn."

"Oh, Ramirez, I wish you wouldn't talk that way. Maybe no one will die. De Vargas is not a man who looks for battle."

"Maybe right about de Vargas, but del Charco also comes."

Sofía drew her breath in sharply. "Del Charco is here?" she asked, her voice almost a whisper.

Ramirez nodded. "He come late last night. He come with fifty soldiers, maybe more. I hear them talk. They come to kill. They not care who they kill...women, children...they insects to del Charco. Insects to be crushed under palm of hand, under hooves of their horses."

I looked down at my breakfast, my appetite suddenly

gone. Ramirez was talking about men who would be wielding death with swinging swords and charging horses. Doctor Lopez hadn't talked about this back in the Great Room. He had said that de Vargas' reconquest had been without bloodshed. Could he have been wrong?

From somewhere out of sight a bell rang. It sounded like a church bell, the clapper striking every few seconds. Then it stopped.

"The meeting will be starting soon," Sofía said. "Carlos, we had better get inside, de Vargas will be expecting you." She turned back to Ramirez. "There are still many things to be decided. Let us hear what the governor has to say before you start worrying yourself to death. I know he will avoid a battle if at all possible."

"I pray you right, Sofía. You go now. I work in kitchen."

He loaded the plates onto the tray and returned through the door from which he had first emerged.

"Poor Ramirez," she said, "life has been very hard on him."

"Because he is half Indian and half Spanish?" I asked.

"Well of course, Carlos. Look at his hair."

"So. A lot of people are bald."

"Yes, a lot of people are bald - but none of them Indian. When he visits the clan of his mother he sticks out like a coyote in a pack of wolves. And he stands out just as bad among us. With his dark skin and squatty build you would never think he was Spanish. At least he was lucky enough to have a father who let him take his name. Most of the *mestizos* don't even know who their fathers are. They are just soldiers who took the women they wanted as they passed through."

The bell rang again and we rose from our chairs. I

followed Sofía into the building, passing the kitchen where Ramirez was now chopping vegetables, and down a narrow hallway that led to a much wider passageway where several people were milling about. Most of them were walking in the direction of a large open doorway at the end of the corridor. Standing on either side of the doorway were two guards dressed in full uniform. Metal armor covered their torsos like sleeveless shirts, and sheathed swords hung from their belts. Underneath the armor, they wore leather vests over white shirts with frilled cuffs. Tan pants made from rough cloth and brown leather boots, like those worn in the common area by the soldiers, came almost to their waist. Skullcaps made from the same metal as their chest armor perched atop their head. The small helmets' shape reminded me of the hats worn by workers behind a fast food counter.

We joined the people who had backed up at the doorway and moved ahead slowly as they pushed through. Sofía and I had just reached the threshold when a gloved hand from behind clamped painfully onto my shoulder and twisted me around.

"Soldiers before children, boy. It will be prudent to learn your place before someone decides to teach it to you."

The words came from a thin pale man with thick oily hair. A straggly beard did little to hide his narrow chin. His thin lips were set in an arrogant smile. He reminded me of a rat in a Saturday morning cartoon. His hand pinched harder causing me to wince in pain.

"What's the matter boy? Don't you know how to address your superior?"

I was about to address my superior with a swift kick in the shin, or places higher up, when Sofía interrupted.

"Excuse us, Captain. We are attendants to the governor, and our bad manners are the result of us not paying attention to those around us. No disrespect is intended."

The pressure on my shoulder slackened and the tip of his tongue passed slowly over his lower lip as he looked at Sofía.

"Well, well, well. Attendants to the governor. I am pleased to see he is not completely lacking in his choice of assistants," he said, running his eyes up and down her body.

"Take a lesson from the young lady," he said sharply, turning his attention back to me. "Perhaps then you will live long enough to sit gumming bread crusts over your gruel and not end up as a spot on the floor sniffed at by passing dogs."

He released my shoulder and the people separated as he sauntered past them into the room.

"Who's that?" I asked Sofía, rubbing my shoulder.

"That is Captain del Charco," she said bitterly. "He is the one Ramirez spoke of. Did you see the way he looked at me? I felt like a lamb in front of a salivating wolf. I would call him an animal, except it would be an injustice to compare him to God's creatures. He is less than an animal. He is a beast from hell."

His behavior and the pain in my shoulder were enough reason for me to take an instant dislike to Captain del Charco, but even so, I was taken aback by her words.

"Pretty strong stuff, Sofía," I said.

"Huh. Not strong enough if you ask me," she said. "You know of his record, don't you?"

I shook my head.

"I thought everybody knew of del Charco. But there is no time to talk about it now, the governor will be entering at any minute and you should be standing behind his seat at the table."

We had passed through the doorway into a large rectangular shaped room dominated by a circular wooden table set in the center. Around it were five uncomfortable looking chairs, one with a higher wooden back marking the head of the table. There were no other chairs, but the base of the adobe walls formed a continuous low bench—called a *banco* in Spanish—that ran along the interior perimeter of the room. A closed door, behind the head of the table, provided a break in the *banco*. Most of the people had finished entering. They were standing about in small clusters and talking in hushed voices. Some had taken a seat on the *banco*.

I followed Sofía as she threaded through the crowd, noticing that each cluster of people had a distinct style of dress. Most were wearing the same uniforms as the soldiers at the door, but without armor. I estimated there were approximately twenty-five of them. The second bunch, numbering about ten, wore coarse blue robes with rosaries draped over cords tied around their waist. The catholic friars Doctor Lopez had described back in the Great Room, I thought. The last small group—there being only three of them—was dressed in much finer clothes than the priests and soldiers. They wore tight-fitting velvet jackets. The word doublets popped into my mind, but I wasn't entirely sure. Some of the velvet jackets were blue and some purple, and all had a thick gold embroidered edge. Their caps had no brim and fit snugly on their heads. They were of the same color and similar design as the jackets. Around their necks were stiff cloth collars that had the texture and fold of an accordion. Their pants were tight fitting and the boots brightly polished. The different clusters seemed to be keeping to themselves, with the exception of Captain del Charco. He had joined the velvet jackets and was talking to them in an urgent manner. They were silent, but listening intently. I noticed that Sofía was the only female in the room.

"We will sit on the *banco* behind the governor's chair," she whispered. "Each of those sitting at the table will have an aide who stands behind them. Lieutenant Montoya will stand as the governor's aide.

"But first everyone has to take their place. You are to stand in front of the door to the governor's office. This will be the signal to the people that they should take a seat. Once they are seated, Governor de Vargas will enter."

"What do I do then?" I asked nervously.

She gave a sigh of exasperation. "I just told you. You come sit next to me on the *banco*. If the governor signals you, then do whatever he asks you to do. Most likely he will not ask you for anything, in which case you do nothing. If the principals ask for anything, it will be as a request through the governor. So just don't do anything until he tells you to."

"There's going to be school principals at the table?"

"What in the world are you talking about?" she asked with an impatient note in her voice. "The men sitting at the table are the principals representing the various interests in the governor's campaign. There will be a representative of the Viceroy, the Church and the merchants. And my guess is del Charco, as the highest ranking military officer after the governor, will also have a seat at the table."

"How about you? What do you do during the meeting?"

"Me? Why, I am the quiet, but pretty, servant girl. I will make sure the cups are filled with water and clean cloths are available for those who have forgotten their handkerchief and feel the need to blow their nose." I smiled at her dry humor and she made a last discreet adjustment to my collar.

"The actors are in place and it is time for the play to begin. Good luck," she said, giving me a gentle nudge toward the table. I took a few steps and glanced back at her. She was still smiling, but her eyes had an apprehensive look to them. I started to turn back to her, but all the people were staring at me. Like Sofía had said, the actors were ready and it was my job to raise the curtain. I squeezed my eyes shut for a moment to clear my head.

It was time for the Council of Governor Don Diego de Vargas to begin.

5

Sage Awakes

In my dream, I felt a soft black pressure weighing upon me. Then I was awake with my eyes tightly shut, and, for a moment, dream and reality were the same. I heard the popping and snapping of burning wood and opened my eyes. The fear that had gripped my heart disappeared when I saw Wise Father add another juniper branch to the flames. The fire was not for warmth, but for the light it shed. I looked at the shadows dancing on the familiar white walls of the room, and touched my hand to the soft lambskin covering me.

I was home, within the walls of the pueblo. Everything was as it had always been.

Wise Father stepped back from the small mud-brick fireplace and slowly lowered his aged body into a cross-legged position on a blanket lying next to the wall. In the weak light of the fire he picked up a small *Katchina* doll and studied it carefully before fixing a small feather to the emerging crown surrounding the face of fluffy white rabbit fur. A sharp hooked beak carved from hardwood stuck straight out from the middle of the face. Small yellow chips of stone formed the eyes and deep, dark pupils painted on their surface stared directly at me.

The body beneath the fierce face was shaped in human form and covered with a multi-colored soft leather vest and skirt. Wise Father worked quickly and the crown was soon complete. The feathers fanned out like the tail of the Great Owl in flight.

"You toss and cry out in your sleep, Sage," he said to me gently, studying the owl in his hand. Then he looked over at me. "Were you visited with a bad dream?"

I pulled the lambskin up to my chin. "I was visited with a dream, Wise Father. It was a dream that seemed as real as the fire burning in the hearth. It has frightened me, but I do not feel it was a bad dream."

"A dream that causes you to cry out, but is not bad?"

"Yes, Wise Father." I closed my eyes and looked back into the dream. The images did not fade, as with most dreams, but instead remained alive and real. "In the dream I am with a brother I love, and who loves me very much. We live together in a square metal box resting on black wheels. It is a comfortable box with soft beds and water that spills into a basin from a shiny metal branch."

Wise Father said nothing, but a small frown joined the many lines on his aged brow.

"In the dream," I continued, "my brother and I help a wise man in his home. It is a beautiful home, with wonderful treasures filling a great room and outside a garden of bushes and trees shaped into many different animals. There, in front of the home, like a guard at the edge of the pueblo, is a large bush formed as the Great Owl."

The frown on Wise Father's brow grew deeper. "That is a foreboding sign to some, Sage."

"Yes, Wise Father. Maybe it is the owl that causes me to tremble. I fear that it is a bad omen, perhaps an omen of death. And when I awake, I find you making the *Katchina* of the owl. Could this mean death is coming to you? Or to our people...or...perhaps to me?"

"Death, and the changes brought with it, will come as they may, Sage. It may be that the owl is a sign of those changes. Whether this is for the better or worse of our people is not clear. However, I do not believe you need fear this unknown. But, tell me more about your dream and what happens at this place?"

"The learned man is perched on a ladder wearing a green cloak. He resembled a..." I hesitated as an image with an unfamiliar name came to my tongue, and then continued. "He looked like...like a gummy bear."

"A gummy bear?" he asked curiously, "What is that?"

"I am not sure, Wise Father," I said with a puzzled note in my voice. "But those are the words that come to me in the dream."

Wise Father nodded his head as if in understanding. "And what happens then?"

"A storm approaches and the owl shudders in the wind as lightning and thunder crash around it. Then a heavy cloth grabs my brother and me like a hand scooping pebbles at the lake shore, and a deep darkness descends."

"Does the darkness recede?"

73

"No, not until I awoke here with you. But in the dream, I know my brother as I know you. How could a dream be so real?"

Wise Father thought for a moment before answering. "Do your eyes not see the dancing of the fire, Sage? Do your ears not hear the sound of the flames consuming the wood? If you put your hand close, do you not feel its warmth?"

"Yes, Wise Father," I said.

"That is because these are things you sense with your outer self. Do you not suppose that your inner self may also sense that which is as real as the light, the noise and the warmth of the flame, but is beyond the sight, sound and feel of what you know to be real?"

"Do you mean that my Dream Brother exists?"

Wise Father lifted the *Katchina* in his outstretched arms until it was level with his eyes. As if in response, from somewhere far outside the wooden door of the room, I heard the distant screech of the Great Owl.

"You hear the call of the owl. Doesn't that mean it is real?"

"Yes, but that is because I hear it with my ears."

"Then perhaps you hear your Dream Brother's call from within. Return to sleep now. Maybe he will visit you again."

I rolled over on my side facing the mud wall. I was wide awake, turning over in my mind the words of Wise Father. It was long after he had gone to sleep and the fire had burned low before I was able to return to my sleep.

There I saw Dream Brother again. He rode on a powerful horse with a blazing star on its forehead. He rode with many men I did not recognize. I watched the changing images for what seemed to be a long time. Then I was wide awake again, shivering beneath my blanket and wet with a sweat like one with a fever. I now knew my Dream Brother's name and that he lived outside my dreams. I also knew he was coming in search of me.

When I woke again, Wise Father's bed was empty. The outside sunlight spilling into the room told me that early morning had passed. My lambskin had fallen to the side, but the nighttime chill had not penetrated the thick mud walls of the room. I rose and made my way through the door and dim entry hall into the plaza. The sweet smell of lavender and freshly baked bread greeted me. A few feet away, Stone squatted on thick, powerful legs in front of his sand pile. He wore no shirt and the muscles in his shoulders rolled like many snakes when he moved his arms. I watched him as he carefully scooped up a handful of sand and let it trickle through his fingers, forming a new pile on ground beside him. By midday, the sand pile would be moved one handful at a time to the new mound. When he had finished, Stone would repeat his movements until the pile was back to where it first lay.

A terrifying mask with wild eyes and a contorted mouth lay on the ground close to his feet. Singing Bird had made it for him during the winter months and it was never far from his side. The ceremonial masks of the Pueblo were not meant for play. But Stone could not be made to know this and many times, to the distress of Wise Father, he would search out their hiding place and then be seen wearing the masks in the plaza. Singing Bird had finally solved the problem by making him a mask of no ceremonial or religious significance that was his own to do as he wished. I do not think Wise Father was happy with Singing Bird's solution, but there was none other that he could offer.

"Good morning, Stone," I said cheerfully, walking up to him and patting his broad shoulder.

His head swiveled around and he looked at me. A gentle smile formed beneath his slightly crossed eyes and his body quivered like a puppy greeting its master.

"Puh-lay?" he asked, struggling to form the word.

"I'd love to play with you, but I need to eat first. I'll come back later." He nodded quickly and turned back to his sand pile.

Stone had seen over forty winters, and he was the strongest and biggest person in the village. However, his mind had not grown with his body. He was unable to hunt or even work in the fields. The most he could do is help the women with their fires, breaking the thicker tree branches across his knee so they were easily handled. Mainly he would spend his day playing with the young children of the Pueblo. When the sun was high and the children napping, Stone would sit in the shade of the pueblo walls with our many dogs sprawled out around him. The dogs wiggled amongst each other to get close to him. Then he would sit patiently for hours, scratching behind their ears or stroking their chests while making small cooing noises in his throat.

I walked past one of the small domed *hornos* that dotted the plaza like brown eggs rising from the ground. Small fires burned inside the mud-brick ovens and a thin trail of smoke carried the delicious smell of baking bread from a hole in the top of the dome. I felt the pinch of my stomach and hurried over to a small table where the other Pueblo children had gathered. I hoped my late morning sleep had not caused me to miss breakfast, but I need not have concerned myself. Deer Dancer, her tiny veined hands tightly clutching a walking stick, stood guard over a platter piled high with squares of cornbread smothered in honey. Resting next to the platter was a large bowl of golden peaches. The children stood waiting impatiently for me to join them. I knew they wanted to begin the morning meal, but their good manners and the stern eye of Deer Dancer kept them in their place.

"Hurry up, Sage," she said with a smile that displayed the last two teeth in her mouth. "Wise Father told me you would sleep late this morning and I should save breakfast until you came. He said you would be hungry from your dreams." I walked up and the other children moved apart, displaying an unusual and curious respect that made me think they knew of my strange dreams.

I took two big slabs of cornbread and two peaches. "Thank you Deer Dancer. I'll take some to Stone," I said, turning from the table. The other children grabbed their portions and followed behind me.

"Want some cornbread with honey, Stone?" I asked when I returned to the sand pile.

"Yuhh," he said.

"And here are some peaches," I said, handing him one of the slabs of bread and both the peaches. I lowered myself next to him with my legs crossed underneath me. The other children sat around us on the sand pile. Nobody talked while we chewed the sweet bread and sucked on the juicy fruit. From where I sat, I could see the older boys and men of the Pueblo working the fields along the river. Wise Father sat close by on a bench next to the wall. With him was Lonewolf, War Chief of the Pueblo. They were deep in conversation. Windsong, a thin girl with straight black hair hanging over her eyes, broke the silence through a mouthful of bread.

"Deer Dancer says you have a Dream Brother," she said

curiously, "and that he is of another place. Are you going to leave us and join him in the dream?"

I started to laugh, but stopped short when I saw the look of worry in her young eyes. The other children had stopped chewing and watched me closely as they waited for my answer.

"I don't think so, Windsong," I said solemnly, though with every passing moment I felt him drawing nearer. He was coming to me in my dreams and soon he would be here. "In my dreams he is riding to meet me," I continued. "After he has come, maybe he will join us and help make sure we have enough corn and meat for the winter."

"Will he play with us like Stone?" she asked.

"I'm not sure. I think if you ask him to, he will. Dream Brother is very nice." I looked away uncomfortably and my eyes met those of Wise Father. He smiled and signaled for me to join him. "Wise Father calls me. I'll be back shortly." They all looked over to Wise Father and the curious respect I felt from them grew stronger. I rose from my place in the sand and walked over to where Wise Father sat talking with Lonewolf.

"Did you want me, Wise Father?"

"I am telling Lonewolf of the dream you had. He has questions that I am unable to answer."

Lonewolf studied me for a moment. He was tall and strong, having seen no more than thirty-five summers, with a manner befitting the War Chief of the Pueblo. The ridges of muscle beneath the skin on his stomach stood out like the curves on the shell of a pumpkin. Angry red battle scars marred the smooth skin of his chest. He had paid scant attention to me in the past, but now his dark eyes bored into me. Then his thin lips relaxed and he smiled.

"I understand you had an uneasy night, that you are

visited with strange dreams that have revealed a Dream Brother to you," he said. "Tell me more about your dream and about him. Tell me how old he is and what he looks like."

I described my dream as well as I could, telling him all I remembered. "My Dream Brother is not a full-grown man yet. He is but a few years older than me. He does not have brown skin like us. In my dream he has a pale skin with tan specks on it, much like a sweet cookie with brown spice sprinkled over the top. His name is Carlos."

Lonewolf gave Wise Father a meaningful look and turned back to me.

"Was that all, Sage?"

"No, Lonewolf. Later, after I had awakened and then returned to sleep, I dreamed of him again. He rode with many men. I believe he comes in search of me."

"The men he rode with, what did they look like?"

"They were not all alike. Some looked like us. I suspect they may be from another pueblo. But, the rest were like none I have seen before. They too were light-skinned and many had red or brown hair growing on their face. They wore vests of shiny metal and swords on their belts."

Lonewolf looked sharply at Wise Father. "It is the Metal People she dreams of," he said grimly. I felt a tremor move quickly through my body as he spoke his words. Lonewolf turned his attention back to me.

"Do you know the place where they were riding?"

"I do not know the place, Lonewolf. In my dream they were riding beside a wide river. Then the river was gone and they rode in heat and dust."

Squeals of laughter and joyful screams interrupted us and we looked over to the sand pile. Stone had donned his mask and was chasing the children around the plaza. He moved with a rolling side-ways gait and bellowed like a bull. The women at the *hornos* had stopped working and were watching the game with smiles on their faces. There was no worry in their eyes. When he caught one of the squealing children, he would pick them up and spin them high in the air, his massive arms catching them carefully. After several tosses, Stone and the child would collapse to the ground roaring in laughter. The scene would repeat itself until all the children had had their turn spinning into the air.

I turned back to Wise Father and Lonewolf. They were deep in quiet conversation. Though I was anxious to take my turn in the air with Stone, I stood patiently until they finished. After a moment, Wise Father spoke to me.

"Is there any more that you remember about your dream, Sage?"

"That is all I recall, Wise Father."

"Then go join the others in play," he said with a smile. Lonewolf gave me a quick tense grin beneath a brow furrowed in thought. I turned to leave, but was drawn back by Lonewolf's earlier words.

"You worry about the Metal People," I said, looking him in the eye, "and your silence cloaks your concern. What do you see in my dream?" He opened his mouth to speak but did not. For a moment, I thought he would rebuke me for my impertinence.

Instead, the words he spoke were gentle. "You know the story about how this became our home?" he asked, with an expansive gesture toward the mud-covered buildings behind us.

"I have heard the stories, Lonewolf," I said. "What we

call Bead Water, and what the white men called Santa Fe, was the center of power for the Metal People. It was built as a place from which the Chief of the white men could rule. Then the great coming together of the Pueblo People pushed from here those who cast the shadow. After their departure, we moved to this place and found our new village."

He nodded his head. "Yes, Sage, that is the story of this place. The white men who ruled called themselves Spaniards. Our people named them Metal People when they first rode up our valley on their big horses. Do you know why they were named so?

"Tell me, Lonewolf," I said in a voice that was almost a whisper.

"Because they clothed themselves in sheets of metal armor that protected them from our arrows and spears. Those whom you describe on horseback with your Dream Brother, and your Dream Brother as well—they are the Metal People, Sage."

My head began to spin and I felt a great weight in my heart. How could my Dream Brother be one of the Metal People? We all knew the stories repeated around the fire during the cold winter months. When I was young they had frightened me, and then later, when I got older, had caused me great anger. Some, like Dancing Deer, would occasionally talk of some of the good that had come to the pueblos from the Metal People. She would talk of the fruit trees and improvements to our fields, and the new God that carried a message of peace and love, and the help the Metal People gave the pueblos in fighting off the pillaging Apache and Comanche. I had to agree with Dancing Deer that they had brought much. However, the memory remained strong in me of the time an elder had

81

sternly asked her the question to which all knew the answer. Could anything brought by the Spaniards be of more value than our lost freedom or the assault on our religion? Dancing Deer spoke no more for the rest of that evening.

"You do not need to concern yourself, Sage," Wise Father said. "Lonewolf will do the worrying for you. Now go join your friends. Stone will be disappointed if you don't play."

I left the two men and walked slowly back toward the sand pile. My thoughts of Dream Brother made me oblivious to those around me, and I jumped in fright when Stone, his face covered by his terrifying mask, leaped out from behind an *horno* with a fearful yell. I tried to run but it was too late. Before I knew it, I was spinning in the air and shrieking at the top of my voice. Then we were rolling on the ground and the other children were running past, skirting close so as to entice Stone into the chase. He jumped up and in a minute had Blue Medicine Flower spinning in the air. Blue Medicine Flower held her legs close together with her feet pointed downward and clutched her arms tight to her chest. I leaned back on my elbows and continued to laugh as she spun higher and higher.

As I watched her, a vision of a woman twirling in the air came into my head. Then I realized it was not a vision, but a memory. In this memory, the woman wore a thin blue dress. The folds of her dress flowed about her like the gentle waters of the river. On her feet were strange moccasins with metal blades attached to the bottom. She glided on the blades above an ice-covered pond in a big room with many people watching. In my memory, I was sitting next to Dream Brother, and we were watching her graceful movements on a small box in our metal home. The image in my mind caused me to stare at Stone with my mouth hanging open in surprise.

How could dreams come to me in the wakeful hours of the day? I began shivering as I tried to understand what was happening to me.

6

Plans of Reconquest

I pulled my shoulders back and walked over to the small door behind the table. As instructed by Sofía, I then fixed my eyes on the opposite wall and stood silently without moving. Immediately four men separated from the crowd and took a place behind the empty chairs. The murmur of conversation ground to a stop and people began to take their seats. A very old friar with rosy cheeks and a clean-shaven jaw took the chair next to the one reserved for the governor. A young priest with a well-trimmed beard stood directly behind the friar. A slender man dressed in a black coat and pants, with the customary white frilled shirt, took the empty seat next to the priest. I assumed he was the Viceroy's representative. His attendant was an older man who rocked back and forth on the balls of his feet while he studied the people in the room. My face remained expressionless, though I felt my jaw muscles tighten, when Captain del Charco took the seat next to the old friar. A huge brute of a soldier, his coat stretched tight over his broad shoulders, stood as his attendant.

One of the velvet jackets—a portly man with heavy hanging cheeks—took the last chair, which put him to the left of the governor's seat. Another of the velvet jackets stood behind him.

The rest of the people found a seat on the *banco*. There were a few last hushed whispers followed by a moment of quiet anticipation. Then the small door opened and I stepped to one side. A man wearing a soldier's uniform stepped through the door. His eyes swept across the crowd, and then, as if satisfied with what he saw, he spoke in a clear deep voice.

"Please rise for Captain General Don Diego de Vargas Zapata Lujan Ponce de Leon, Governor of New Mexico of the Kingdom of New Spain."

Everyone stood and clapped politely as the governor entered. He was dressed like the soldiers, but the cut of his uniform and quality of the cloth made theirs appear shabby in comparison. He was a slender man with a bearing that reflected the stature of the high office he held. He had a close-cut beard and mustache, and his thin dark hair hung down to his shoulders. His dark eyes glanced around the room. There seemed to be a natural twinkle in his gaze, as if what he saw before him was a source of amusement known only to himself. His eyes rested for a moment on Captain del Charco and his huge attendant. For a moment the twinkle disappeared—replaced with a hard icy flatness that made del Charco shift uncomfortably. The twinkle returned as the

Governor moved slowly from guest to guest, addressing each by name and taking a moment to exchange a few words.

Then his attention turned to those at the table, again greeting each individually and trading a few words as he went from chair to chair. When he reached his place at the table, he gave me a wink and took his seat. The soldier who had announced his entrance stood behind him. In a single fluid motion that reminded me of a church service, the people all took their seat. I sat next to Sofía in a space she had saved for me.

"How am I doing so far?" I asked in a low voice.

"Wonderful," she whispered back with a hint of a grin on her face. "You stood up and you sat down. I was amazed by how skillfully you managed the task."

I gave her a withering look, but before I could make a smart come back, Governor de Vargas leaned forward in his chair, clasped his hands together on the table and started to speak.

"Welcome, my friends," he said, "and thank you for journeying to El Paso del Norte on such short notice. I have no doubt that the wise counsel you provide today will help guide us as we prepare for what can only be described as an historic campaign. I know many of you have ridden long and hard to be with us, and your efforts are much appreciated." He looked over at Captain del Charco and nodded his head. The captain returned his nod with a smile, but his eyes smoldered with undisguised anger.

"Thank you, Governor," he said through clenched teeth. "It was only yesterday that we heard of the Viceroy's orders, and made due haste to assist you in your planning of the reconquest."

"Unexpected help is always welcome, Captain," the governor responded.

"Huh," said Sofía under her breath, "in other words, the governor was hoping to have the meeting without del Charco's knowledge. But now that he is here, he has to be included."

"Why doesn't he just tell him to take a hike," I whispered back, "He is the governor after all."

"Take a hike?" she asked, not understanding my choice of words.

"Why doesn't he just tell him to leave," I said. Her confused look disappeared and she shook her head.

"He can't do that. Protocol won't allow it. He is stuck with him and there is nothing he can do about it right now. Maybe later he will figure out how to rid himself of that devil."

"We have much to contemplate today," the governor continued, "but before we discuss the king's directive, let me, as the first order of business, introduce the principals so that all should know the wisdom and experience each brings to this gathering.

"Captain del Charco is, I believe, well known by reputation and deed to those who have followed his many brave forays into New Spain during the time before and since the Pueblo rebellion." He looked directly at del Charco. "I know, Captain, that you may be...uh...how would you say...put out because I did not invite you here personally. I assure you that no slight was intended."

Del Charco gave a small nod toward the governor. "I'm sure it was but an oversight in these busy times. Think nothing of it." He smiled again, but his eyes remained cold. De Vargas didn't seem to notice and continued to speak.

"And behind the captain is his aide, Lieutenant Campos."

Campos gave a curt nod of his massive head in the governor's direction. He had a blank, lifeless look on his face, but in his eyes I sensed a rage just below the surface. The huge scarred hands hanging at the end of his muscular arms might have been chiseled from chunks of granite.

I felt Sofía shudder beside me and I bent my head toward her. "His nursemaid?" I asked. The corners of her mouth tightened.

"More like his attack dog. Just make sure that when del Charco snaps his fingers it is not in your direction." She leaned closer and spoke so low that I could just make out her words. "It is said that there are some undertakings so reprehensible that even del Charco's black soul shies away. For those tasks— for those unspeakable tasks—he calls upon Campos."

His hulking presence combined with Sofía's words sent a chill through my body. It reminded me of something that had once happened when I was dropping flyers for Carlotta. One of my stops had been a house with an enclosed screen porch in front. Bushes surrounded the porch and stepping into it was like entering a cave. I quickly stuffed the flyer in the space between the front door handle and threshold. Then, as I turned to leave, I sensed a presence in the murky darkness. It was big and black and moving slowly in my direction. The figure took shape and there, not more than a few feet in front of me, was a giant Rotweiller. I gave an involuntary flinch and it stopped moving. It stood like a show dog, its muscular legs spread wide, and looked at me through shiny unblinking eyes. I talked to it in a low voice, calling it a nice doggy and asking it if it wanted a bone, while I backed away slowly until I was through the screen door. I had been startled when the dog appeared out of nowhere, but what really frightened me was the sense that at any time a tremendous and devastating force could be released by the slightest provocation. I had the same feeling now as I stared at Campos.

De Vargas studied him silently for a moment and then turned to the old friar. "Father Marcos," he said, "I am honored to have such a high ranking emissary of His Holiness seated at this gathering. Your inspiration and counsel is much desired."

"Thank you for your warm words, Governor de Vargas," Father Marcos said in a raspy voice. "It is good to be back in New Spain. Though I enjoyed my assignment at the Vatican—Rome is such a beautiful city—ten years is a bit too long of time to be away from the place I consider my true home."

"For those who don't know, Father Marcos, prior to the revolt, had spent most of his life in the northern territories, in Santa Fe, bringing Christianity to the Pueblo people," the governor said. "By the grace of God, he was traveling in Chihuahua when the revolt took place."

"And by the grace of God I will live long enough to return to Santa Fe after you have successfully completed the reconquest. I only wish I could accompany you now, but I am afraid that this old body would be more of a burden than a help. My attendant, Father Chavez, will travel with you in my stead."

De Vargas nodded his head as the priest spoke. "I fear your assessment is correct, Father Marcos. It will be a long hard march through difficult terrain. And at the end of the march we may find ourselves engaged in battle. But the wisdom of your many years is of more value than the strength of a hundred soldiers. As one who lived among the Pueblo dwellers, your insight is of special significance and value."

"I am here at your pleasure, Governor," the old priest said. "As is my way, I will speak my mind and will put forth my best advice. Whether you take it or not is your choice. But if you choose to not heed my words, then the lost souls of the Pueblo People will be upon your head when you meet our father in Heaven."

A murmur ran around the room at the old priest's words. Father Chavez, standing behind Father Marcos, flushed a deep shade of red and a pained look came to his face.

"Boy, he sure doesn't mince words," I said to Sofía.

She shook her head. "No," she whispered, "Father Marcos not only speaks as one whose time in this world grows short, but also from the frustration born of his unfulfilled mission in the pueblos.

I thought de Vargas would get angry or at least be taken aback, but instead he allowed a small chuckle to escape his lips and he gave a deep nod that was almost a small bow to Father Marcos.

"Father, the lines on your face and brashness of your tongue are all the reason I need to weigh your words most carefully. I will do my best to heed your advice." De Vargas turned his attention to the old priest's aide. "Father Chavez, your joining with the company eases my worries. I will consult with you regularly."

"I am at your call, Governor. Though none can replace Father Marcos, I will do the best I can."

"Thank you, Father," de Vargas said. He then looked over at the man in black seated next to Father Marcos. "It is our pleasure to also have seated with us at the table the personal envoy of the Viceroy, Octovio Garcia y Delgado. Welcome, Señor Garcia y Delgado."

"The pleasure is mine, Governor," Garcia said with a pleasant grin. De Vargas returned his smile and turned to the man in the velvet jacket sitting to his left.

"The Pueblo Revolt caused much damage in many different places," he said, "Luis de Oca comes as a representative of those whose commercial enterprises were lost in the revolt. Welcome, Señor de Oca."

De Oca acknowledged de Vargas' greeting with a few flaps of his hanging cheeks. De Vargas continued to stare at him expectantly. Finally, after a few more flaps, he spoke.

"Governor, we are pleased that this campaign is now finally set to begin. Too much time has been allowed to pass since the savages took what we worked so hard to attain. What we have lost shall be ours again."

I heard a small snort come from Father Marcos' direction and saw that the old priest was staring at de Oca with anger in his eyes. De Oca either didn't notice, or chose to ignore the father. I didn't think that de Vargas had missed it.

"Yes, what was lost shall be regained," de Vargas said absently, "but we must ensure that that which we lost was really ours to lose."

De Oca squirmed a bit in the uncomfortable looking chair and flapped his cheeks again, but he remained silent.

"What is that about?" I asked Sofía.

She looked over at me with a curious look. "You are playing with me, Carlos. Everyone knows what the merchants would like to see." I shrugged my shoulders and gave her a blank look. She let out an exasperated sigh. "They want the Pueblo Indians to be like chattel. In their minds, the Indians should be considered no different from the oxen that pull the plows or the horses that carry them about their estates." I could tell from the tone in her whisper that she didn't think much of the velvet jackets.

Governor de Vargas took a sip of water from the shiny brass goblet in front of him and cleared his throat. He looked slowly around the table as if studying each of the council participants and weighing their various needs and the value they brought.

"Can you believe, my friends, that it is already twelve years since the Pueblo Revolt occurred. Twelve years since the Indians of the Northern Pueblos descended on the King's settlements like a pack of dogs on their master. The killing was wanton—men, women, children—it made little difference; all were fair game to the Indian warriors. Homes were torched and the churches defiled, the priests slain at the altar. Some four hundred colonists and twenty-one friars met a violent death at the hands of these people.

"Though only twelve short years ago, it is now an important page in history. On the other side of the Atlantic, the loss of one of the King's outermost frontiers has caused a great deal of consternation in his court. The Crown does not lose the territory of its empire, but instead expands upon it. The image of Spain's soldiers fleeing from savage Indians has created a loss of face in the eyes of the world that goes beyond the significance of the revolt itself. Hence, since the day the news of the revolt reached the King, the Viceroy has been under orders to retake the northern territories.

"And an unsuccessful attempt was made. The Viceroy allowed Governor Otermin, under whose administration the revolt occurred, the opportunity to reconquer New Spain. Otermin failed in his attempt, and the Viceroy appointed me Governor." De Vargas reached again for his goblet. Del Charco took the opportunity to break in.

"Excuse me for interrupting, Governor de Vargas," he

said, emphasizing the word Governor with a hint of scorn, "but I think it important that all in attendance be aware that I too was considered by the Viceroy for the governorship. In fact, I have it from very good sources in Mexico City that it was only after much deliberation that you were chosen over me, and that the political authority you command is tenuous at best."

De Vargas's eyes narrowed, but the tone of his voice remained unchanged.

"Perhaps the Viceroy's representative, Señor Garcia y Delgado, would care to address your remarks," he said.

Garcia y Delgado stroked his short beard and paused before answering. "There is some truth in Captain del Charco's words. His military exploits in the field qualified him for the post."

He paused again, choosing his words carefully. "Unfortunately for the Captain, those same military exploits are the reason he is not leading this important mission."

Father Marcos made another snorting noise, or maybe it was a stifled laugh, I wasn't quite sure. I noticed that some of the people in the room were smiling, while others stared at del Charco with repugnant expressions on their faces. I turned to look at Sofía. She was staring at me with an expression that said, 'Didn't I tell you so.'

Del Charco's head shot up at Garcia y Delgado's words and he glanced around the room in a menacing fashion. When he spoke his voice was strained. "I will not," he said. "I repeat, I will not apologize for my conduct at Cloud City. One of the Indians in the village killed a soldier. The whole village had to be punished with pain that would not soon be forgotten. I acted in the manner of a soldier of the Spanish Empire and carried out my duty as I saw fit."

"Therein lies the problem," said Garcia y Delgado coolly, "and the main reason that de Vargas was appointed governor instead of yourself. It is not the intent of the king to beat the Indians into submission."

Del Charco's face flushed the color of a plum and his lips quivered in anger.

"The Pueblo Indians are subjects of the king, and are not to be treated with undo brutality," Garcia y Delgado continued. "Governor de Vargas' reputation as a fair and tolerant man fits well with the king's wishes in this matter and I think it unwise to question the political support he enjoys. The Crown is well aware of the strategic value our outposts in the northern areas provide, but the real mission is to reclaim Spain's honor and save the savages from their uncivilized belief in pagan Gods."

Del Charco opened his mouth to speak again, but Father Marcos quickly spoke first.

"With all due respect to the Viceroyalty, saving those Indian souls is what brings me here today, Señor Garcia y Delgado," he interjected. "Over the years before the revolt, our friars had done a commendable job in bringing Christianity to these people. We had many converts, but, unfortunately, while many accepted Christ as their savior, they still continued to worship the imaginary spirits of their religion. It is God's work that we do, and turning them from their traditional pagan ceremonies is a part of that work."

Father Marcos paused and signaled to Sofía for more water. She went quickly around the table filling the cups and returned to her seat next to me. "What if they don't want to be turned?" she whispered. "What if they are happy with the religious beliefs they have?" I didn't think she wanted me to answer, which is just as well since I didn't have one.

"However," Father Marcos continued, "the history of the revolt records that the Pueblo Indians singled out the church's chapels for destruction. Obviously there was resentment to our activities that we were blind to.

"The reconquest, Governor, must be done in such a way that the Indians' souls are saved and a strong religious bond with the church forged."

De Vargas listened carefully as Father Marcos spoke. Del Charco, for his part, had slumped down in his seat and was glowering at the table. I looked at him, curious about what he had done at Cloud City that had cost him his appointment as governor. He must have felt my stare. Abruptly his head swung around and his dark cold eyes met mine. I shuddered and quickly looked over at the velvet jacket, Luis de Oca, who had begun to speak.

"Father Marcos's concern over these savages' souls is commendable," he said in his deep baritone voice, "but we cannot forget the important role these people played in the areas of commerce before the revolt." Father Marcos snorted again, and de Oca shot the old man an irritated look.

"This is a poor country and the colonists were producing barely enough to subsist when my associates and I arrived," de Oca continued. "We organized the labor force and were producing textiles and goods for export. When the revolt came, we were forced to leave without our equipment, our workers or our—"

"Workers? Labor Force?" Father Marcos interrupted loudly. "Don't mince pretty words! Call them what they were!"

"I'm sure I don't know what you mean," de Oca said haughtily.

"You know very well what I mean. You and your followers

had these people in virtual servitude. You took the blankets they wove and gave them almost nothing in return. And then you demanded more. The so-called workshops you established were stinking hell-holes worse than most jails."

"We paid them wages," de Oca responded in the tone of the unjustly accused.

"You mean you promised them wages. Wages they never saw. The concept of money was alien to these people. When you assured them they need only have their names in your ledgers to receive compensation, they believed you. Then the passing weeks turned to years and they still received nothing. Nothing! Yours and those like you would fill the wagons and head back to Mexico City. The Indians were left here with years gone from their lives. They had nothing to show from it and with almost no recourse available."

De Oca's cheeks flapped faster and faster as the old priest spoke. Then he sat up in his chair and looked down his nose at Father Marcos.

"There may be something to what you say, Father," de Oca said stiffly. "But can you rightfully condemn our actions in light of the church's behavior."

De Oca's response seemed to have hit a nerve. The anger showing in Father Marco's eyes faded and he leaned back in his seat, his shoulders slumped.

"Of course, you are right," he said flatly. "The methods we adopted to save these people from their traditions were horrendous in their own right. As I said, we turned a blind eye to the effect of the changes we wrought upon the Indian way of life. We now know why they singled out our places of worship during the revolt." He glanced around the room. "It was because we singled out theirs. With the soldiers behind us, we marched into their *kivas* and systematically destroyed that which they held sacred. The *kivas* themselves we left in ruins. They were punished like common criminals—worse than common criminals—if we discovered them practicing their native religions. We whipped them, put them in the stocks and, in some instances, hanged them. And we did it with impunity. The church was the judge.

"And then there are the beautiful churches that we constructed on the backs of these people. Physically, they are small men. But we would herd them like cattle and take them fifty miles to the mountain forests. Then back another fifty miles, this time carrying the massive logs needed to support our ambitious construction efforts. We were so intent on building these houses of worship that we would forget the message of peace and love that is the cornerstone of our religion."

Father Marcos finished speaking and the room was silent. Father Chavez stared down at his clenched hands as if in silent prayer. Del Charco's harsh voice finally broke the silence.

"I suppose this baring of the soul has some cleansing purpose," he said. "But let not the sentimentality of the moment distract us from the purpose of this council."

"On the contrary, Captain, these are the thoughts that are so desperately needed at this time," de Vargas countered. "All truths must be on the table as I plan the reconquest."

"These are not the truths that we need, Governor," del Charco said. "The only truth we need is the acknowledgment that this is a military campaign. And it is a campaign that will only succeed through military prowess. The soldiers gathered outside this room are at your command. Use them to bring terror to those that oppose us. Let us march forward and crush any signs of rebellion. Yes, many men on both sides of the conflict will die, but only then will you secure for yourself a place in history as the conqueror of this remote Spanish frontier."

"You may be right, Captain," de Vargas said thoughtfully, "but there is something to be said for being remembered as a leader of men, rather than the butcher of Indians."

"Then let me take the soldiers and you follow behind us. I think your position dictates that you be kept from harm's way. Once we have subdued the savages, you can march in and raise the Spanish flag again."

"Captain del Charco," the governor said, "I will lead this campaign—let there be no doubt about that. All the soldiers, including you, will be under my direct command. I will expect my orders to be followed and I will decide when and how we move against the Pueblos. And, Captain, a peaceful reconquest is the preferred method of the Crown and myself. Is that understood?"

"Yes, Governor. I will do my best to insure a peaceful campaign," Captain del Charco said with a sneer on his face. "You are the governor and I am here to serve as you see fit."

Governor de Vargas studied him silently for a minute. It seemed as if he was ready to court martial him where he sat—high rank or not. But instead, he chose to ignore him and turned his gaze back to the people in the room.

"Our march to Santa Fe is not to be taken lightly, doubly so in the heat of summer. My aide, Lieutenant Montoya," he said indicating the soldier standing behind him, "is responsible for the logistics of the move. We will hear from him first, and then let those who have traveled the Northern Territory tell us all that they know of the journey."

Lieutenant Montoya briefed us on the latest information

coming from Santa Fe. Apparently, the Indians, after having routed the Spaniards, took possession of the government offices, called the Palace of the Governors, and converted them into a Pueblo where a group of *Tewa* Indians now lived. The outside walls had been reinforced and the large rooms within divided into a virtual maze of many small ones. The company would have at their disposal two cannons capable of breaching the walls of the palace. This would allow the soldiers to enter with a direct frontal attack, but it would be at the cost of many lives—perhaps as much as half the company.

The room was silent when he finished. I glanced at the two armored soldiers who had remained standing at attention on each side of the entry. I figured they weren't much older than Sofía. A sobering thought hit me. If Lieutenant Montoya was right, and I had no reason to doubt he wasn't, then one of them had only a few weeks of his young life left to live.

The phrase 'dead man walking' came to mind.

The governor stirred in his chair and signaled to an older soldier sitting on the banco across from him. The soldier quickly rose to his feet and began describing the route the company would travel. Crossing the deserts of New Mexico was brutal by any stretch of the imagination. Fortunately, the Rio Grande, which ran from southern Colorado all the way to the Gulf of Mexico, paralleled the trail, called the *Camino Real,* for much of the journey. I felt my eyes open wide, however, when he told of the ninety-mile stretch called *Jornada del Muerto,* the Journey of the Dead. During that part of the journey, the company would be forced to leave the river and travel northward across some of the most inhospitable areas of the Southwest. It got its name from the many people who had perished in the almost waterless passage.

After the soldier finished his frightening presentation, plans were made for gathering the provisions needed to feed the men and water the oxen, horses and cattle that would be making the trip with us. De Vargas proved his skill as a manager with pointed questions and comments. When the strategies of the journey were complete, Governor de Vargas spoke.

"Is there anyone else who would address this council?"

All were quiet.

"Then prepare to march. Please give Lieutenant Montoya any assistance he may require. We leave on Thursday, a week from today."

With that, the governor pushed back his chair and stood. Everyone else took to their feet, and a moment later they were speaking to each other in quiet but animated conversation. De Vargas turned and spoke to me for the first time.

"Interesting times, eh, Carlos," he said almost nonchalantly, but with a worried furrow above his brow. "I want you to help Lieutenant Montoya prepare for the march. You assist him in whatever he may need. When we leave, you will be traveling with me."

"Yes, sir," I said, overwhelmed by what was happening around me.

He must have detected the uncertainty in my voice. His eyes, which seemed to be staring at something unseen in the distance, focused on me.

"You're not scared, are you?"

"No, sir," I lied.

He gave me a little smile. "Well, you should be," he said. "I know I am."

7

On the *Camino Real*

It took three days to carefully load the massive wagons with the supplies that would sustain us during our crossing of the *Jornada del Muerto*. What a name, I thought, Journey of the Dead. It sounded like something out of the *Goosebumps* books I used to read back when I was a kid. Like some of the things in those books, the macabre name sent chills down my spine.

The sun was coming up over the rocky hills to the east just as I finished securing the last of the wooden barrels. They were empty now, but would be filled with water from the Rio Grande River when the company turned east and began their march through the *Jornada*. Stacked in front of the barrels were sacks of dried corn and jerked beef for the men, and bales of hay for the oxen pulling the wagons and the horses carrying the soldiers. The hay, which would supplement the native feed along the *Camino Real*, would also feed the steers brought along for butchering.

I jumped down from the wagon and wiped the sweat off my forehead on the sleeve of my shirt. It was going to be a hot day, just as it had been all week. I would have bet that the temperature had gone at least a few degrees over a hundred each day.

During the week, Lieutenant Montoya had stood over us from morning to night. He was a nice man who had the makings of a good ground crew supervisor in a busy airport. He carried a sheaf of crumpled papers listing all the preparations for the march. Newly forged iron horse shoes were tacked to the animal's hooves, with replacements for those broken or thrown during the march packed into a wooden box on one of the wagons. The wagon wheels were inspected and re-inspected and rations for the men and animals carefully secured. He left nothing to chance—even the soldiers' packs were inspected, with Lieutenant Montoya tossing out anything he thought unneeded.

Sofía kept busy doing what she called 'textile transformation.' In fact, she had proven herself to be an expert with needle and thread. I guess some people would have called what she did woman's work, but it was much more than that. Need new soles for your boot? No problem, bring them in and in a few minutes they were as good as new. A steady parade of soldiers brought her packs and saddles that had outlived their usefulness, but, in her skilled hands, were brought back to life. Lieutenant Montoya assigned me to help her when she worked in the stable. I was not only to assist her, but I was also to learn as much as possible about the art of leatherwork. Riding equipment would tear or fail during the long journey north. The company needed someone skilled in the repair of leather equipment, and that someone would be me.

During our long hours in the stable I picked up bits and pieces of our past together. And what I learned almost floored me.

Sofía and I were survivors of the Pueblo Revolt.

I had been five years old and Sofía seven when the revolt occurred. My family—a family I never knew existed—and hers had settled on their farms in the Española Valley. When the Indians attacked, all the families in the valley took refuge in Sofía's home, hoping at any moment to see Spanish soldiers riding to their rescue. The soldiers never materialized and, like the rest of the settlers, our families decided to flee to Santa Fe. Unfortunately, a large band of roving Indians gave chase. There was only one horse among the settlers and, as the Indians closed in, Sofía and I were placed in the saddle and sent galloping toward Santa Fe. The families we left behind were not heard from again and were presumed dead. After that our upbringing alternated between a string of other colonial families and the Church.

It was no wonder that Sofía felt as close to me as she did. As for me, the only thing that kept me from sitting down and laughing or crying—I'm not sure which I would have done— was the numbing effect this whole weird dream, or whatever it was, had already had on me. Instead of saying anything of this remarkable life I'd never known, I simply kept my mouth shut. Given the circumstances, it seemed the smartest thing to do.

Now, after a hard week of preparation, there was an atmosphere of excitement and anxiety as the march began. The horses seemed to feel it too, straining at their leads while the mounted soldiers struggled to keep them in place. The oxen pulling the monstrous wagons snorted and shuffled back and forth. I stood in front of the caravan next to an Indian who held the reins of the horses that would carry the governor and Lieutenant Montoya.

I'd become acquainted with my own horse during the week. She was a strong brown mare with a splash of white shaped like a star on her forehead. From this mark she took her name, Estrella. Unlike the other horses, she stood quietly and watched with an attentive eye. I had never ridden a horse before and I was more than a little nervous our first time out. Watching the soldiers, I had at least seen how to saddle and mount her. Once in the saddle, it was simply a matter of tugging the reins in the direction I wanted to go. Most of the soldiers wore cruel-looking metal spurs, but it just took a little pressure from my boot heels to send her into a gallop. When I wanted her to stop, I would pull the reins in tight. Other than that, the mare pretty much did everything else herself. I walked over to where she was tethered to one of the wagons. She looked at me with her big brown eyes while I scratched her behind the ear.

"Hey, don't you know you cannot be a *Conquistador* without a sword," a now very familiar voice said from behind me. I turned to find Sofía staring at me with a shy smile. In her hands was a new leather belt looped through a black metal scabbard. A small cord secured the shiny metal hilt of the sheathed sword.

"I didn't know I was a *Conquistador*," I said, returning her smile. "I thought I was just an attendant."

"You ride next to the governor. When you are in battle, the enemy will not see a difference between an attendant and a warrior, nor will they care if there is one," she said. "Here, take it." She thrust the scabbard and belt at me, but her eyes did not meet mine.

"Thank you, Sofía," I said softly, taking the belt and loosening the cord. I pulled the sword from the scabbard. It was about two feet long with a thin narrow blade. I tested the edge with my finger. I could have shaved my few whiskers with it.

"It's not really a sword, more like a long knife. I figured for someone of your build it would be easier to...to use."

"It's the perfect length. The leatherwork is beautiful, Sofía," I said, staring at the tiny patterns etched into the belt. Then I did a double take. In the center of the belt was the small image of a tree. It was too small to make out clearly, but it sure looked an awful lot like the tree on the tapestry outside Doctor Lopez's office.

"Did you make it yourself?" I asked.

She nodded, her eyes still fixed on some point just below my chin.

"When did you have time to do this? You were working on everything else all week."

"You don't think I can make a little time for the one who would run to me when he had scrapes or cuts to be bandaged? Or needed me to help pull his boots on because he was trying to force them onto the wrong feet? Or," she asked in a ragged voice, "or, cry my name in the middle of the night after a bad dream?" Then a tear ran down her dusty cheek to the corner of her mouth. Suddenly I felt a lump in my throat and a stinging in my eyes. I swallowed hard and cleared my throat.

"Don't cry, Sofía. Everything's going to be all right," I said awkwardly.

"Crying? Who's crying? Not me," she said, wiping the back of her hand across her cheeks and finally looking me in the eye. She stepped forward and gave me a tight hug. "I'm going to save your chores for you. There will be a lot of work waiting, so you make sure you hurry back as quickly as you can."

"I will," I said. She released me and gave me a light peck on the cheek. Without another word, she turned and walked back toward the building that housed the governor's office.

Even though I told her I would be back, I wasn't so sure. It had been almost a week since I found myself in El Paso, and every morning when I woke I half-expected to open my eyes and see the familiar surroundings of Doctor Lopez's Great Room or the ceiling of our trailer back home. I knew I couldn't possibly stay asleep long enough for the dream to take me all the way to Santa Fe. Maybe it would even be over before I got to the nightmare place called the *Jornada del Muerto*.

At least I hoped so.

There were other times, I have to admit, when I couldn't help but know that it wasn't a dream. Everything around me was so real. And, if it wasn't a dream, then what had happened to Sage when the lightning struck? She was never far from my thoughts, and Sofía's talk about bandages and scrapes and cuts had brought her back to the top of my ever-growing list of worries. For the millionth time I wondered if she was walking around in this time and place. I had kept my eyes open for any sign of her during the past week, but had seen nothing that even remotely suggested she was in El Paso. Even so, for some reason I couldn't explain, the feeling that she was somewhere close got stronger and stronger with the passing of each day.

Well, there wasn't anything I could do about it now. I

was on my way to conquer my home town of Santa Fe.

I put on the belt and scabbard. It felt a little strange against my leg when I led Estrella away from the wagons and kept banging my knee when I tried mounting her. Finally, after three tries, I made it. It was a good thing Sofía had given me a short sword, otherwise I would have needed a chair every time I wanted to climb in the saddle.

With my feet securely settled in the stirrups, I looked around to see what the rest of the company was doing. Just about everyone had mounted their horse or climbed onto a wagon. Most of the men were staring at the point in the middle of the melee where Governor de Vargas and Lieutenant Montoya walked slowly among the soldiers making their final checks.

I watched as the governor exchanged a few words with one of the wagon drivers. Like all the other drivers, the man he spoke to was an Indian. I'd been surprised at the number of Indians who were making the journey with us. There was almost twice as many of them as there were soldiers. In addition to driving the wagons, they would tend to the animals and make camp at the end of the day. When I commented to Sofía about their large number, she called them friendly Indians. This meant they had sworn allegiance to the Spanish flag and to King Charles, who sat on the throne across the Atlantic Ocean in Spain. After working next to them for a week, I had decided that the term 'friendly Indian' wasn't accurate. They were plenty friendly when they were among those of their clan or tribe. They laughed and joked and had animated discussions in a language I didn't know. But, when they spoke with a Spaniard, it was as if an invisible shutter was drawn across their eyes, keeping in any emotion or glimmer of their thoughts. I became uncomfortable working alone with them, at first because I felt like an outsider, and then later because of the hidden animosity I sensed toward all Spaniards. They may have sworn allegiance to the King, and were considered Spanish subjects, but they were not, by any stretch of the imagination, happy campers. I was pretty sure that if they had their way, they would be waiting out the heat of the midday sun in the patched shade of one of the scrawny trees, instead of moving and lifting heavy boxes loaded with provisions for the journey.

I peered over the back of one of the strings of oxen and caught Father Chavez's eye on the other side of the square. He gave a wave, which I returned. Four other priests had joined him for the march. They were all dressed in their traditional blue robes. This had also surprised me. In all the pictures I had ever seen of Franciscan Priests, the robes were always brown.

There was no sign of any velvet jackets. They would not be joining in the campaign, but would return to Santa Fe if the governor returned from a successful reconquest. What a bunch of chickens, I thought, avoiding the danger and then grabbing their take when everything was safe.

Del Charco and his aide, Lieutenant Campos, had left the day before. The governor had sent them ahead to gather intelligence about Pueblo activities. It was hoped that they could provide an early warning if hostile Indians were waiting along the trail. I was just as glad that the two of them wouldn't be riding with us. My dislike for the captain had turned to revulsion when Sofía told me the chilling story of what occurred at Cloud City when justice was served del Charco style. It had happened before the Pueblo Revolt, and, according to Sofía, it was one of several incidents that helped rally the Indians when they finally decided to act together and boot the Spaniards out of New Mexico.

It had all started when a small group of soldiers traveled west from Santa Fe on an exploratory mission aimed at finding the Pacific Ocean. When they reached Cloud City, so named because of its location on top of a tall rock outcrop, an Indian from the Pueblo had descended and killed one of the soldiers. When word of the attack reached the then governor in Santa Fe, he had sent del Charco to return the rebellious Indians back to the cloak of Spanish rule. With a company of seventy soldiers, del Charco marched to the Pueblo and in a ferocious battle subdued its people. I suppose that would have been the end of it if he had stopped there, but del Charco decided that an example had to be made as a warning to any Indians who would dare challenge the soldiers of the Crown.

He had Lieutenant Campos and the other soldiers under his command round up all the men of the Pueblo who were over twenty-five years old. The captured Indians were bound and taken to a small trench dug in the ground. There, screaming, pleading and yelling for mercy, they were held down by del Charco's soldiers with the lower part of their right leg suspended over the trench. Del Charco's main man, Lieutenant Campos, then straddled the ditch, raised his sword and slashed down on the Indians' ankles, severing their foot from the leg. By the end of the day, the trench was filled with the brutally amputated feet and del Charco had obtained his objective: the Indians subjected to this horrific punishment would never pose a threat to Spanish soldiers as they spent the rest of their lives hobbling around with only one foot.

But, del Charco was not content with stopping there. He then had his soldiers take twenty young girls from their Indian parents and send them five hundred miles south to Mexico where they lived in virtual enslavement. Sofía had shuddered and I had cringed when she described the treatment the girls suffered from the soldiers during the long trip south. When the Spanish government learned of the cruel punishment administered by del Charco, they held a tribunal and stripped him of his command. However, he was allowed to remain as a soldier, and, over the years, had regained and surpassed his previous rank, making him the highest ranking military officer after the governor.

I had been surprised that del Charco could have made such a comeback. When Sofía told me the story, I just figured that was the way things worked in the seventeenth century. Then, when I considered some of the things I had learned in my history classes, I realized that even three hundred years doesn't change some things. The twentieth century has also had its own share of people who seemed to have gone down the tubes, but then—in a stunning turn around of fortunes—re-emerged in positions of enormous power. Two examples popped to my mind. John F. Kennedy beat Richard Nixon in their race for President, and then Nixon lost again in his try for governor of California. Yet six years later Nixon was President of the United States. Even Adolph Hitler, whose first try at garnering power landed him in jail, returned to conquer most of Europe. I guess del Charco's court-martial and subsequent comeback to such a high-ranking position should not have come as any big wonder.

I didn't have time to think about that at the moment. De Vargas had climbed up on his big gray stallion. I quickly kneed Estrella over to my place behind him. He raised his right hand above his head and held it for a moment, then in one graceful movement brought it down to where he was pointing ahead, and started his horse forward. Like a train engine moving from the station, our military convoy lurched forward. Stealth would be out of the question. The creaking wagons and snorting horses probably could be heard for a mile, and the dust we threw into the air could be seen for several more.

The path north to Santa Fe was called *El Camino Real*: The Royal Road, or alternatively, the King's Road. Though it carried a noble name that conjured up in my mind images of a well-made road meandering under tall leafy trees, the *Camino Real* was in actuality a series of several trails and wagon ruts. In some places, the trails had been cut deep by rainwater runoff. When a wagon encountered one of those areas, it simply moved over a few yards and started a new set of tracks that would form the road until the next rain came. The soldiers gave their horses little direction and allowed them to select the trail they preferred.

The slow moving water of the Rio Grande formed a natural boundary to the road on the west, while a flat open plain stretched off to a distant mountain range in the east. Scraggly green mesquite bushes, prickly cactus and tufts of stunted yellow grass grew wide apart in the pale looking soil. The only signs of wildlife were the occasional jackrabbit and some quick moving lizards.

We rode without stopping until the sun was directly above us. Then the caravan took a break and rested. Our lunch was a plate of pinto beans, the rich juice sopped up with hard brown bread. Afterward, we continued to ride. By the middle of the afternoon I was shifting uncomfortably in my saddle as the inside of my upper legs began to rub raw from the constant back and forth motion of the horse. The soldiers were wearing the same type of armor and skullcaps I had seen earlier. I had been hoping to get my own set of armor during the week before we left, but as an attendant I wore the same clothes Sofía had so painstakingly prepared for the meeting of the council. Now, as I watched the sun beat down on the metal and saw the sweat dripping from the soldiers' faces, I was glad to have only my cotton shirt between me and the occasional cool puff of wind that blew across the river.

It was late afternoon when we finally stopped for the day. I climbed stiffly down from Estrella and unhitched the heavy saddle. With a muffled groan, I slid it off her back and lay it on the ground. She shook herself like a dog coming out of a bath. The hair on her hide was drenched with sweat where the saddle had been pressed against her. I handed the reins to one of the Indians who was gathering the horses to take to the river for watering and gave her a pat on the rump before she was led away.

A few yards from me Governor de Vargas dismounted and handed his reins to another Indian. I had ridden next to him for most of the day, but he had spoken little, and what he did have to say was mostly to Lieutenant Montoya. Now he sent me off in search of Father Chavez with an invitation to join him for dinner. I found the Father and other priests about a hundred yards downstream. They were warming a small pot of beans over a fire of driftwood plucked from the banks of the river. As I walked up, Father Chavez was dropping pieces of squash and dried meat into the beans.

It seemed Father Chavez was expecting the governor's invitation and he accepted it with a smile. From the deference accorded the father during the past week, I had come to realize that though de Vargas was the military leader of the reconquest, that leadership was shared with the priest. As a man of the cloth, the soldiers of the company looked upon Father Chavez as a sort of icon of spiritual hope. With so much uncertainty ahead, he provided a confidence of faith that helped boost the soldiers' morale.

In many ways, it was not much different than what I had been told of the Pueblo Indians and their own priests. I guess this was one of the similarities Doctor Lopez had spoken of back in the Great Room.

By the time I arrived back at the governor's camp, the sun had dipped below the horizon and the temperature, though still hot, was almost bearable. Father Chavez joined us a few minutes later and, after a short prayer, we started eating. When we had finished, an Indian appeared and took our plates. The governor and the priest continued discussing the day's events and seemed oblivious to the Indian's presence, though they both gave me a curious look when I said thank you as I handed him my plate.

I leaned back against my saddle while the governor and father sat crossed legged on their saddle blankets. The soldiers and Indians had formed into small groups around the fires dotting the riverbank and the low buzz of their conversation mixed with the soft watery sounds of the river. To the left of us, outside the ring of light thrown by our fire, I could make out a solitary soldier sitting alone on the riverbank. The moon hung above the horizon, and the soldier seemed transfixed as he stared over the water at it.

"You set a good pace today," Father Chavez said. "I would guess that we covered over twenty miles."

"It was a good pace, Father," the governor said in agreement. "If we can maintain it, we should be in Santa Fe within a month."

"And then, Don Diego?" the Priest asked. This was the first time I had heard the governor referred to so familiarly, but de Vargas didn't seem to find anything strange about it. He stared into the fire and was slow in answering, as if looking to find an answer in the dancing tongues of flame.

"I don't know, Father Chavez," the governor said. I noticed he did not call Father Chavez by his first name. "I just don't know. It is not realistic to hope that the Indians will welcome us in the same manner as they did the first Spaniards almost a century ago. Then they offered us food, shelter and friendship. Now I fear their welcome will be in the form of spears and arrows. And, if that is what the future has in store for us, then I will have no choice but to do as del Charco has recommended. We will descend on them with all of our might. When it is over, they will either be a vanquished people, or we shall have perished."

"Perhaps. But you must consider, Don Diego, that your actions determine what the future holds. The transformation of the Pueblo Indians from friends to foe did not happen overnight. That, at least, was made patently clear during our meeting. What you do, and what you say, will be the foundation upon which subsequent generations of Spaniards and Indians build."

"I am well aware of that, Father. But, like you, I have my mission to complete. You must bring the church, and I, the Spanish flag to this land."

I watched Father Chavez nod his head slowly in agreement with Governor de Vargas' words. While they talked, I felt a growing sense of being watched. I looked into the darkness toward the river. My night vision was shot from looking into the flames of the campfire, but after a moment I was able to make out the silhouette of the solitary soldier sitting on the bank. I couldn't tell if he was looking our way.

"You are of course right, Don Diego," Father Chavez continued, "but perhaps together we can offer accommodations that will allow us to complete our mission while at the same time bringing peace between ourselves and the Pueblos."

"Accommodations?"

"An example, Don Diego. I am here to bring Christianity to the Indians. But if the church forbids them the practice of their own religion, then the animosity I encounter will make it impossible for me to be successful. So I must ask myself, how do I overcome the animosity? The answer is quite obvious. The church must turn a blind eye to their native rituals. Then, and only then, will we find them receptive to the teachings of the gospel."

"You cannot be serious, Father Chavez," the governor said with a note of surprise in his voice. "Is the bishop aware of this...uh...accommodation you are suggesting?"

"I have discussed it privately with his Grace. He will make no official decree concerning this issue, but he is in agreement that peaceful co-existence is necessary for us to go about our work. It is of course our belief that once the word of God is received, the Pueblo Indians will no longer have the need of their native spirits, and our missionary work can then be a success."

Governor de Vargas gently stroked his beard with the back of his index finger and considered what the priest had told him. I continued to stare at the soldier next to the river. I was convinced that he was watching me. Maybe I was being paranoid, but I didn't think so. I've always been able to feel when someone is staring at me. Mom kids me about it sometimes, calling me a telepathic. I don't know about that, but my internal radar was so focused on the soldier that I missed the first part of what the governor was saying.

"...and the church will acquiesce if I make that policy?"

"If you mean that I, as the voice of the church in New Mexico, will agree to offering the Pueblos religious freedom, then the answer is yes," Father Chavez said, rising to his feet stiffly. I wasn't the only one who was sore from the day's ride. "I hope that I have been of some use to you in planning your strategy, but it is now time to take my leave and get a good night's rest."

The governor also rose to his feet and rather absent-mindedly thanked the priest for joining him in dinner. I could tell he was turning around in his mind the possibilities that had opened with what he had been told. I stood up and the father and I wished each other good night. After he had left us, the governor gave a huge yawn.

"Are you ready to call it a night, Carlos?"

"If you do not mind, Sir," I said, "I think I will try to walk off some of the stiffness in my legs before I go to bed."

"That's fine. It will take a few days for all of us to get our riding legs. Just don't wander too far from camp and watch out for rattlesnakes," he said with another yawn. He lay down on his saddle blanket and pulled another blanket over his shoulders.

I walked a few steps from the fire and looked over at the soldier still sitting silently by the river. I was curious about the watcher and decided that the best approach was a direct one. Stretching out my arms behind my back, I moved nonchalantly in the direction of the water. Up above me thousands of stars shone bright in the clear desert sky. In their light, the soldier's outline became clearer as I got close. The profile of the soldier's face looked familiar—and no wonder, considering that I had spent a lot of hours looking at it during the past week.

"Holy cow, Sofía, is that you?" I whispered.

"No, it's the Queen of England, and don't call me a cow," she said in a low voice. "Of course it's me. I was beginning to think you were going to talk all night. Come on, let's walk up the river a ways where no one can hear us."

I followed behind as she made her way carefully up along the river bank. From behind she looked like any one of the soldiers in the company. Her long brown hair was hidden beneath the metal helmet on her head. When we had moved beyond the sleeping groups of the company, she stopped and turned to me.

"Okay, ask your silly questions and get it over with. I'm here for the duration unless you give me away."

Oddly enough, I didn't have any silly questions. I was just happy to see her.

"That armor suits you well," I said.

"You think?" she said, holding out her arms and giving a small curtsy. "I believe it will become the latest style for the ladies of the king's court. How can the soldiers wear this? I felt as if I were in a cooking pot all day. And this stupid helmet has given me a headache that would knock a bull to the ground."

I laughed at the indignant tone of her voice.

"You think it is amusing, do you?" she continued. "We shall see how amused you are when you have to wear it."

"Me? Why should I wear it? It looks perfectly fine on you."

"Because I brought it for you. I have just borrowed it so that I would fit in with the other soldiers. When I am found out, which hopefully will not happen until we have crossed the *Jornada del Muerto*, I will then rid myself of it. It will fit you perfectly."

117

"Why can't you be found out until after the *Jornada*?"

She gave a sigh of exasperation and spoke to me as if she were explaining something simple to a little child. "Because then I will be able to continue on the journey northward. The governor cannot send me back across the *Jornada* by myself, nor can he just leave me. He cannot spare any of his soldiers so he will have no choice but to take me with him."

"You want to go to Santa Fe that much?" I asked.

"I don't want to go to Santa Fe at all. But I am not going to be stuck with your chores into perpetuity just because you happen to march naively into the spear of a Pueblo Indian. And I know that is what is will happen if you are left to your own devices."

"I can take care of myself."

"Ha! You can't even mount your horse with a sword on your belt. I watched you this morning. It took you three tries to get on Estrella."

"Uh, you saw that?" I asked, feeling an awkwardness I couldn't really explain.

"Yes, I saw that. And I also watched you riding Estrella. If I didn't know better, I would have thought you had never ridden a horse before. And I also have watched you do some things as if for the first time, though you have done them a hundred times before. You also do this with the people you know. Sometimes you act as if you are meeting them for the first time. I've seen old people forget things, even the faces of those who have been around them all their life. But you are too young to be suffering from whatever it is that makes them that way."

Her words were more a question than a statement and I saw a curious and worried look in her eyes. For a moment

I hesitated, debating whether to tell her the truth. There was nothing to lose as far as I could tell. She probably wouldn't believe me and might think me crazy, but she couldn't say anything to anyone without revealing her true identity. She was the one who had to move about in the guise of a Spanish soldier. More than anything else, I felt the need to confide in someone. Living in this strange place and time, not knowing how long I could be here and my concern for Sage were taking a bigger toll on me than I probably wanted to admit. I grasped her armor-covered shoulders in my hands and looked her straight in the eye.

"That's probably because I've never ridden a horse before, Sofía, and I have never met anyone here until just before the council meeting," I said in a steady voice. "I know you think I've been with you since I was a child, but all I really know is what I have learned since you woke me up the morning of the big meeting."

She didn't say anything for a moment. Then she put her hand on my forehead.

"Well. You don't have a fever," she said softly.

"I'm not crazy, Sofía. I don't understand it either, but a little over a week ago I was having Thanksgiving supper, in my home, in a time that is three hundred years in the future."

"Thanksgiving? Three hundred years in the future? Carlos, don't tell me that one day's march on the trail has completely addled your brain."

I sighed. "My brain is not addled, Sofía. Or at least I don't think so." I started to explain Doctor Lopez and the Great Room and the antechambers, but realized that whatever I said would be completely foreign to her. "I don't know what is going on. I do know that I am here for some reason that probably has to do with de Vargas' reconquest." I hesitated for a second, then plunged ahead. "And I'm pretty sure that I'm not here alone. I also think my sister, Sage, is here."

"Carlos, you don't have a sister," she said.

"Not here I don't, but back where I came from I do. And she was right next to me when this all started. She is somewhere here all right, but I haven't seen her."

"Maybe she is disguised as a soldier like me," Sofía said with a note of disbelief in her voice.

"No, I would have spotted her if that was the case," I said matter-of-factly. "She is not with us, but she is still here in this time."

"Carlos, you are talking like one possessed," she said, making the sign-of-the-cross. "Maybe I should let de Vargas discover my true identity now so I can take you back to El Paso. We can put you in a bed away from the hot sun."

"It is not the sun that is making me tell you this," I said, choosing my words carefully. "I know it sounds crazy, but I am from a New Mexico that has long been settled. The Pueblo Indians are still there, and so are the people who will be born from these soldiers and the settlers to come. I'll be a descendent of the soldiers and settlers. My father's family can be traced back to Spain."

"That is not so incredible. All the people here have family back in Spain," she said.

"The reason they have ties to their families in Spain is because they have been on this side of the ocean for less than a hundred years. What I'm talking about are ancestors that have been dead for centuries." I hesitated for a moment.

"And, I'm beginning to think that my sister and me being here has something to do with the reconquest."

120

Sofía started to reply but was interrupted by a voice that came from the darkness behind us. "I think, that instead of talking and keeping the coyotes awake, you should both be snoring in your bedrolls."

"Wise words, Governor de Vargas," Sofía said, disguising her voice by dropping it about three octaves. "It will be a long day tomorrow."

I could feel Governor de Vargas studying us carefully, and I wondered how much of our conversation he had heard.

"We were just noting the beauty and brightness of the stars, but it is time to watch them from my bedroll," Sofía continued in her baritone pitch. "So I shall wish you all a pleasant night and be on my way." Sofía turned and moved quickly into the shadows.

Governor de Vargas watched for a moment as she walked quickly away and then turned to me. "Who was that soldier, Carlos? He looks familiar, but I couldn't quite place him."

I hesitated for a second before answering. I've told a few fibs in my time, but I really don't like lying. Half the time you have to embellish the first lie with more lies until finally it gets so complicated you can't keep track of what you have said. I also worry about what people will think of me when they discover I wasn't telling the truth. Sofía had already told me that she planned to reveal herself after the *Jornada del Muerto*, which meant that if I lied to de Vargas now, he would soon know the truth. But I had given my promise to Sofía, and saw no choice. So I told a small fib.

"Uh, I believe he said his name is Private de la Sofas," I said.

"De la...?" he said questioningly. In the darkness I couldn't make out the expression on his face, but I could have sworn I detected a note of amusement in his tone.

"Sofas, Sir." I said finishing his statement. "Private de la Sofas."

"Hmm. You know, I don't recall anyone named de la Sofas."

"I believe he arrived just yesterday with the last of the soldiers from Mexico City." Just as I expected. A second lie to help support the first.

"Oh?" he said, as we moved back toward the campfire. "Well he certainly cuts a fine figure in that armor, but he doesn't walk like a soldier. Did you notice how he didn't seem to move quite right?"

"Probably just sore from the horseback ride," I said.

"Probably so," he agreed.

I decided it was time to change the subject. "I thought you had retired for the night, Sir?"

"I thought I had too. But Father Chavez has given me much to think about. The church's willingness to let the Pueblo Indians practice their native religions has provided me with an important tool in our reconquest. I must reconsider my strategies and use this new policy carefully. There are many separate parts to a campaign, and one can never know exactly how they will affect the outcome." He gave a thoughtful pause. "I am still incredulous that the church would demonstrate such tolerance."

We arrived back at our campfire, which had burned down to a bed of glowing embers. Most of the camp was asleep. Beyond the sleeping forms, I could make out the silhouettes of the guards posted to keep watch. They would be rotated every few hours so they could get some sleep. I would have to take my turn some time, but luckily not tonight. Tonight I could roll up in my blanket and sleep until morning. In a moment I was on my back trying to make myself comfortable. I stared up at the star-studded sky, reminding me of the image of the painting hanging in Carlotta's café, and felt the heavy weight of my eyelids. As they slowly closed, my mind went back to Doctor Lopez's collection of Catholic crosses and Indian masks. Like the governor, the doctor had also brought up tolerance. I thought about his telling Sage and me of the peaceful co-existence that the Spaniards and Indians would come to share in the future. Governor de Vargas had hit the mark when he said the role church tolerance played could affect the outcome. He had also said there were several parts to a campaign, and some uncertainty with each part.

I fell asleep wondering what, if any, my part would be.

8

The *Jornada del Muerto*

We reached San Diego a few days later. It wasn't the San Diego of southern California with its sandy beaches. There were no homes or people here, just a wide grassy plain rising gently from the river. The oxen and cattle roamed freely, munching contentedly on the thick grass and building their strength in preparation for the arduous journey ahead. While the animals grazed, the company rested in the shade beneath the cottonwood trees that grew along the banks of the river. This San Diego was the last resting-place before we began our march through the *Jornada del Muerto.*

During the first days of our journey north from El Paso, we had followed the bank of the Rio Grande. Looking back from San Diego, I could still see the sharp peaks of the Organ Mountains rising above the eastern bank of the river. The spear shaped pinnacles layered against each other like the overlapping teeth of a great white shark. The steep slopes seemed barren of vegetation and looked like an alien backdrop in a science fiction movie.

By the end of our second day at San Diego, Governor de Vargas was impatient to begin the crossing of the *Jornada*. Everything and anything that could hold water was filled to the brim. All the animals were taken to the river one last time and the governor ordered the men to drink until they could hold no more. By the time we were ready to start, the evening shadows had crept upon us. But that was okay. The governor's plan was to avoid the strength sapping heat of the day by traveling through the *Jornada* during the nighttime and early morning hours.

Governor de Vargas, mounted on his horse, finally gave the signal to start. Some of the wagons wheels stuck in the loose sand where the grass hadn't taken hold and the oxen had to strain on their leads to get them rolling. In a short while the column of soldiers and wagons, followed by our small herd of cattle, was moving slowly toward the *Jornada*.

It didn't take us long to get there.

Within the first half-mile after leaving the river, we had moved from the thick grassy plain and magnificent cottonwood trees to stunted scrawny mesquite brush and yuccas with white, bell shaped blossoms sprouting from the middle of the cactus. The only grass was little tufts clinging to the north side of the low, steep hills. Soon the hills disappeared and we were riding up a wide, dry valley. To the east were the San Andres Mountains, and to the west the Caballo Mountains. The waters of the Rio Grande flowed on the other side of the Caballos. To reach the river, we would either have to return to our starting point at San Diego, or, as planned, push forward until we had passed the length of the mountain range, eventually skirting an immense black volcanic rock plain called *malpais* by the early Spaniards, and then, finally, through Lava Gate to Fray Cristobal on the east bank of the Rio Grande.

Twilight came, and with it a peaceful calm that seemed to muffle the sounds of the tramping animals and rumbling wagons. Sofía was riding a few dozen yards behind me and I fell back from my position next to the governor until I was alongside her. She rode alone and slightly apart from the main body, allowing us to talk freely in low voices.

"How are you holding up?" I asked, letting Estrella find her way around a huge monster of a yucca with green protruding barbs that were twice as long as the blade of my sword.

"I am in need of a long hot bath, but I would have settled for a dip in the river at San Diego."

At San Diego most of the company, including myself, had stripped naked and dunked themselves in the tepid water of the Rio Grande. Sofía had stayed back and discreetly averted her eyes while the men washed themselves with the harsh soap we carried in our packs. It had been refreshing, and I felt sorry for her.

Being disguised as a man also posed other problems. One time, while in the shadow of the Organ Mountains, she told me she thought her kidneys would suffer irreparable harm while she waited for the darkness that would allow her to disappear into the shadows unseen.

"You didn't miss much. The water was cold and muddy with prickly weeds growing on the bottom," I said in a weak effort to console her.

"Huh! I noticed that neither the cold and muddy water

126

nor the prickly undergrowth kept you from floating on your back for almost an hour," she said with a slight note of irritation in her voice. "So don't be trying to tell me how awful it was."

I cringed slightly. "You saw that, huh?" I asked, trying to remember how far away she had been while I was drifting leisurely, without a stitch on, in the slow moving waters.

"Yes, I saw....that," she said, smiling at my discomfort. "But don't worry. I didn't see anything that was particularly interesting." I could feel my face turning red and hoped she wouldn't notice it in the fading light. Before I could say anything more, one of the soldiers moved within hearing range, and I was spared from having to continue the uncomfortable conversation.

The last tinges of the red sky to the west disappeared. Soon we were riding under the light of the half moon. The governor kept a steady pace through the night, with a brief rest every two to three hours. I watched the moon set at about two o'clock that morning, and we continued with only the dim illumination of the stars showing the way.

In the murky darkness, mesquite brush and rocks jutting up out of the landscape sometimes seemed as if they were Indians silently watching us. The shapes were so lifelike that on two occasions a small contingent of men was sent to investigate and make sure they really were rocks. Uneasiness gripped the company, and I sensed a feeling of relief when the sky turned from black to gray with the coming of the new day. An hour later the sun had cleared the horizon. And an hour after that everyone was wishing for the return of the cool nighttime air.

The temperature rose quickly and the back of my shirt became wet with sweat. By mid-morning the air was shimmering from the heat rising from the barren earth beneath us. My mouth was dry and I licked my lips in an effort to keep them moist. That didn't help much so I took a few small swigs of water from the sheep bladder hanging on my saddle. The water had a dank taste to it, but even so I had to fight the urge to take huge mouthfuls and gulp it down quickly. It wasn't an easy thing to do, but the thought of running out of water in this hot and dry land helped me keep that urge in check.

The arid landscape passed slowly, and I was wondering how much further we would ride before stopping for the day. I knew our goal was to reach a resting-place called *Perillo*. One of the first groups of Spaniards crossing the *Jornada* had named it after a small dog traveling with them: *perro* being the Spanish word for dog. According to what I was told, the colonists making up the caravan heading into New Mexico had exhausted their water supply by the time they arrived at *Perillo*. While they were contemplating their miserable fortune, the dog had pranced into camp with a muddy snout and a wet coat of fur. Backtracking along the damp trail of doggie footprints, the Spaniards discovered pools of water left in hollows of the desert by a recent rain, and the caravan was saved.

As the sun climbed towards noon, we reached *Perillo*, but the depressions that had held water for the colonist eighty years earlier were dry. We continued on from *Perillo* for about another hour, but by this time the horses had begun to stumble with fatigue. Finally, Lieutenant Montoya raised his hand, signaling the company to stop.

We watered the animals for the first time since we had left San Diego. The company had no choice but to use the water in the barrels in the back of the wagons. I had never thought a horse, or a cow for that matter, could hold so much water. By the time they had finished watering, our reserves were half gone.

Everybody knew we had hoped for water at *Perillo*, and an air of gloom had descended upon the company when we came up dry. To make matters worse, one of the soldiers made a grisly discovery while we were making camp. He had been sent to secure the area outside of the camp perimeter. He'd only gone about a hundred yards when he suddenly began calling urgently to Lieutenant Montoya. Several soldiers, myself included, hurried over to see what he had found.

The first thing that caught my eye were the sun bleached skull and bones of a horse. Wrapped around the skull was a crumbling leather bridle with the still intact reins tied to a large mesquite bush. A weathered saddle lay on its side where the muscles of the horse's back had once been. A few yards from the saddle lay the smaller bones of the rider.

The governor and Father Chavez joined the growing group of men. The priest looked upon the scene for a few seconds and then lowered his head in prayer. Governor de Vargas ordered a grave dug. When it was finished the company gathered round and watched as the bones of the rider were gently placed into the hole in the ground. The grave was filled with dirt and Father Chavez held a brief service.

It was a somber group that walked away from the burial. I heard some of the soldiers speculating that the dead man had probably been riding from the south, and had arrived at *Perillo* with the same expectation of finding water. Only he hadn't had the reserves carried by the company. In my mind I saw the exhausted rider desperately looking over the dry terrain and the foreboding range of mountains sitting between him and the Rio Grande. And then the final realization that neither he nor his horse could finish the last part of the journey, forward or across the mountains, to the waters of the Rio Grande. Instead of going on, he had decided to wait, gambling that the wisps of clouds floating in the blue sky above would join together and deliver a rain that meant the difference between life and death. But the rains hadn't come, and he had lost his gamble.

After the burial, we spent the midday hours dozing in the shadow of the wagons. There was no shade to protect the animals, and they stood listlessly, swaying slightly on their legs, while the harsh sun beat down on them as it made its slow journey across the sky.

The company, as it had done the previous day, continued the march in the late afternoon. The waning moon shed less light than the night before. The good thing was that it didn't set until almost four o'clock in the morning, which meant we only had a couple of hours of total darkness. When we stopped the next morning it was at a resting-place called *Aleman*—the Spanish word for German. We did not expect to find water there, and our expectations, unfortunately, were met.

On a small hill to the east of the resting-place was a row of graves marked with wooden crosses in various stages of deterioration. According to Lieutenant Montoya, it was the burial site of a small group of Germans who had been making the trek up the *Jornada* to Santa Fe when they were descended upon by a band of Indians.

None had survived the attack.

With all our well-armed soldiers, it was highly unlikely that we would experience the same fate as the Germans. But I could tell that the thought of the men who had perished in such a harsh and violent manner, coupled with our find at *Perillo*, weighed heavy upon the company.

By the time the animals finished watering at *Aleman*, our reserves had fallen dangerously low. The next place we could hope to find water was about twenty miles ahead at *Laguna del Muerto*, which translated into Lake of the Dead. Talk about another confidence inspiring name.

And, in fact, my confidence was just about gone. As I tossed and turned, trying to catch a few hours sleep beneath the wagon shielding me from the mid-day sun, I wondered again and again what kind of craziness had put me into this situation. In the movies I would be the stoic hero marching forward toward a noble goal, and then at some point in the story the goal would be reached and everything would turn out okay. But that was the movies, and this lunacy had to be accepted as reality: a reality where my sun-bleached bones would probably be joining those of the Germans, and the man and his horse, on the *Jornada del Muerto*. Maybe someday I would be buried with a few prayers and some speculation as to how I had met my end.

I dismissed that morbid idea. What I had to do was keep pressing forward in the hope that my strange journey back through the centuries was not meant to end with the pat of a shovel on a loose pile of dirt covering the tip of my nose. "Are you stout in spirit?" Doctor Lopez had asked me. Now I knew the meaning of his question, but I no longer knew for sure if I had given him the correct answer when I had said yes.

There was a definite slackening in our pace when we began our afternoon march. Several hours later, about halfway through the night, I noticed that my awareness of the surroundings had dimmed considerably. The shadows from the rock formations, the occasional sounds of an animal scurrying through the bush, and even the horses and men around me had taken on an almost dream-like quality. Then I realized that there were no conversations taking place, and the usual bawling of the cattle and whinnying of the horses had ceased. Exhaustion from the heat and lack of sleep, coupled with dehydration, had taken its toll on both man and beast.

We should have made it to *Laguna del Muerto* shortly after sunrise, but at our slower speed, we didn't reach it until almost noon. From far away, the large, low impression in the ground shimmered like a welcome oasis in the desert. The soldiers and wagon drivers pushed their animals harder, but as we moved closer the water seemed to evaporate. It had been a mirage. The only moisture to be found was in the damp dirt below the cracked dried soil. Thick tufts of grass and tall weeds grew where water from a summer rain had filled the *Laguna* several weeks earlier. At least the animals could fill their stomachs and draw a little moisture from the plant matter before we set off again.

Finding no water at *Laguna* meant we could not replenish our reserves until we reached the banks of the Rio Grande at the end of the *Jornada*, still some fifty miles away. I don't think the company's morale could have sunk much further. The men moved like robots as they made camp. There was very little talking, and the light bantering that had been common place at the beginning of the march had disappeared.

Again, we had no choice but to use the water reserves. The men formed a line and we were permitted two cups each from the barrels. Long shallow wooden troughs were pulled from the wagons and placed on the ground to water the animals. Then the barrels were tipped almost on their side until most of the remaining water splashed into the troughs. Lieutenant Montoya watched closely, and when there were but a few inches left in the barrels, he abruptly signaled for them to be brought upright. The men stepped back and the animals rushed for a place at the trough. There was much pushing accompanied by loud sucking noises as they gulped down the water. In less than a minute it was gone, though the animals continued to lick the troughs as they tried in vain to pull the last drops of moisture from the pores of the wood.

Neither the men nor the animals had drunk enough to satisfy their thirst. My tongue felt heavy and my cracked lips were soon dry again. I still had about a cup of water left in the bladder tied to my saddle, and I was sorely tempted to drink it down. But I knew as bad as my thirst was now, it would only get worse once we resumed our march.

I caught a glimpse of Sofía at one of the other troughs. Her horse had finished drinking and she was gently scratching its forehead and whispering softly into its ear. We hadn't been able to talk much lately, but whenever our eyes met she would put on a smile that said 'Everything is fine, no problems here.' But things weren't so great now, and I saw the worry in her face.

Later that afternoon, when the company had finished preparations, Lieutenant Montoya ordered the men to assemble in front of a flat rock about the size of a kitchen table. Governor de Vargas stood in the middle of the rock with Father Chavez to his right and one of the younger soldiers to his left. The young soldier gripped an unfurled yellow silk banner in his hand. A hot breeze blew from the south, causing the flag to flutter. For a moment I could clearly see the magnificent lions and the scarlet royal castles embroidered onto it.

The three men stood silently on the rock until the sounds of movement and talk died down. When it was quiet, the governor spoke.

"We have traveled fast and far over the past days," he said in a matter-of-fact voice, "and I compliment each of you on the strength and courage you have exhibited. I fear, however, that our first battle is upon us, and our enemy is not one that we can vanquish with the force of arms. I will not try to deceive you. I had hoped that here at the *Laguna del Muerto* we would find the water needed to sustain us as we completed the crossing of the harshest part of our journey. But fate has dealt us a cruel blow, and we are left with no option but to put our faith in God and continue our trek with the same courage that has brought us this far. To do otherwise would be a cowardly act of despair—despair that is unknown, and foreign, to soldiers of the King.

"For we must remember, in this land so far from Spain, that our company is the outermost boundary of the empire. With each step we take," he said, gesturing toward the flagman, "the flag of the Spanish realm takes a step with us. A mere three days ago, the domain of his Majesty, the King, ended south of here at San Diego. Today it rests at *Laguna del Muerto*, and, by tomorrow evening the flag will fly on the banks of the Rio Grande at *Fray Cristobal*. God travels with us, and upon him we shall find the strength to ride forth from this abysmal land."

The soldiers and Indians nodded their heads and stood straighter as they heard the governor's words. Their slack jaws tightened and I saw a glimmer of hope come to their eyes. Governor de Vargas stood back and Father Chavez took his place in the middle of the rock, bowed his head and asked the men to join him in silent prayer.

We bowed our heads. After a few minutes, Father Chavez looked up and made the sign of the cross. The company did the same, and we returned slowly to our horses and wagons.

With a small groan I pulled myself up into Estrella's saddle. My legs were sore from the chaffing of the leather saddle, and my tongue still felt like a dry piece of leather. But I also felt a small burst of energy that seemed to clear my brain of some of the turmoil that had been active there. Around me I heard bits of conversation that reflected a change in the soldiers' spirits.

Again we started like a train leaving the station. The flag bearing soldier, Governor de Vargas, Lieutenant Montoya and myself were the locomotive, while the rest of the company fell in as we left the *Laguna del Muerto*. Within a short time, the long string of soldiers, carts, and cattle were moving behind us.

We plodded along for quite a while, and then, long after the sun had set, the company stopped for a short break. I heard the governor telling Lieutenant Montoya that he didn't want the men and animal's muscles to tighten up. Our rests would be quick and widely spaced until we reached the river. He was afraid that if we stopped for too long, the animals would balk at moving again. A few minutes later we continued our march and the night passed slowly. The rhythmic swaying of Estrella's walk brought a flow of thoughts that drifted back to Mom and Sage. It had been more than two weeks since I woke in El Paso, and two weeks since Mom would have left work to pick us up at Doctor Lopez's. She would be out of her mind with worry when she found the smashed window and disheveled ladder, and no sign of Sage or me. What could Doctor Lopez tell her? I felt sure he would try and reassure her in some way. But the last I saw of Doctor Lopez, he was hanging from the gutter while lightening and rain crashed around him. Maybe Mom found him limp and unconscious next to the hedge. What if he was dead, struck down by the same bolt of lightening that had tossed me across the floor?

Mom is about as tough as they come. I'm not sure if

she was always like that, or if being on her own with two kids to raise had made her that way. I remember Sage coming in through the door of the trailer with a deep and gory gash on her leg after a wreck on her bicycle. She was as pale as a ghost and could barely stand. I also remembered another time, back in third grade, when some of the other kids and I had been playing football in the street in front of our trailer. A sixth grader had delivered a particularly hard block that had thrown me to the pavement. When I sat up my arm was bent back at an impossible angle. It had hurt like hell and was even scarier to look at. Mom had come running out of the trailer when I started screaming at the top of my lungs. On both occasions she had quickly taken charge of the situation in her stern no-nonsense way. Towels had been packed against Sage's gash, and, in my case, a splint tied to my arm before she took us to the hospital emergency room. Mom had taken care of all crisis situations without missing a beat. Panic and tears were foreign to her.

But having both her children missing was totally different. I could see her rushing into Doctor Lopez's home and dialing nine-one-one, then standing helpless while the police tried to figure out what had happened. Even if Doctor Lopez knew where we were, they would never believe it. For all I knew, at this very moment she was sitting at home next to the telephone waiting for some word from the police or hospital telling her that we had been found. I saw her sitting bent over on the couch, clutching her knees and slowly rocking back and forth like the day that Dad died.

I was so deep into my thoughts that I hadn't noticed Sofía pulling her horse up next to me until she spoke a second time. "Hey, did you hear what I said or do you have too much dirt in your ears," she said softly.

"Huh? Sorry, my mind was someplace else. What did you say?" I asked dully.

"I asked how much water do you have left. My water bag is almost full, do you want a drink?"

"Uh, no. I still have a little left. How come you still have a full a bag? From what I can tell, everyone else's is about empty."

"I guess clean living and good planning," she said lightly, but I noticed that her speech was thicker than usual. Even in the weak light of the quarter moon I could see dark circles underneath eyes that seemed to have sunken deeper into their sockets. If her bag was almost full, that meant she had had no more than two or three cups of water in the last twenty-four hours.

"No offense, Sofía, but you're not looking to good. Maybe you better take a drink" I said.

"I'm feeling fine," she retorted.

"Sofía, you're not going to do anybody any good by dying of thirst on us."

She hesitated again before speaking. "I feel fine, but will it make you feel better if I take a little sip?"

"It will make me feel much better."

She looked at me and then nodded. "A little sip does sound kind of refreshing right now." I watched as she lifted her water bag and took a small drink. After a moment she tilted the bag and took a longer swallow. "Aaah," she said, "the water tastes so awful but feels so good flowing through my parched mouth. Are you sure you don't want a drink?"

Of course I wanted a drink, everybody wanted a drink, but I wasn't going to help myself to the water she had so carefully saved. "No, I had enough at the *Laguna*."

"I have always known when you are fibbing, Carlos. Go ahead and have a drink."

"Maybe later, Sofía," I said.

She nodded and we rode for a few minutes in silence. "You were so deep in thought when I rode up," She said. "What were you thinking about?"

"I was thinking about my home."

"Back in El Paso?"

"No, Sofía, my home three hundred years from now."

"It scares me when you talk of this, Carlos," she said. "This is real, not whatever strange thoughts you may have."

"Yes, this is real, but no more real than what I have left behind."

"Tell me about what you have left behind."

"Now?" I asked.

"Why not? Do you have something more pressing to do?"

I drew a deep breath. "I guess not," I said, trying to figure out where to start. Then I just let it spill out. I told her about school and my life in the trailer park. I explained how things were different from today. I told her about my life with Mom and Sage. Maybe I was rambling, but, like she said, I had nothing more pressing to do as we rode up the *Jornada del Muerto* with the shadows of the cactus around us. When I had finished I looked at her and wondered if she was going to laugh, or maybe call Governor de Vargas over to lock me up for the remainder of the campaign. But what she finally said took me by surprise.

"Carlos, I don't know what to believe anymore. Two weeks ago I was living a life completely foreign to what is happening to me now. My biggest worry was making sure the bed linens were washed and the bread was baked. Tonight I must contemplate the fact that I may be living my last day in this world. And, if we should reach the river and make it to Santa Fe, I have to face the fact that in all likelihood I will witness a violent fight that may very well leave you, or me, or both of us dead. And, even if we should overcome the Pueblo's resistance, many of those around us will not come out alive. I have no choice but to prepare myself for bloodshed, and, unfortunately, I know the violence won't be confined to soldiers and warriors, but also to the women and children of the Pueblo. But a part of me refuses to accept that something that atrocious will ever become part of my life. If that part of me cannot accept such a reality, then how can I hear what you have said, and be so certain that your words are untrue? At the very least, I believe that in your mind the story you have told me is as you believe it to be."

"Thank you, Sofía," I said.

"For what, Carlos? For thinking that what you have told me is no more crazy than what I find happening around me?"

"Yes, that too, but also for being here and letting me unload on you." I paused for a moment and watched the lines of worry that had formed above her brow. "Sofía, it will make you feel better to know that every year, in the Santa Fe of my time, the city has a huge *fiesta*. It is a three day celebration held to commemorate Governor de Vargas' reconquest of the city. And, it is a celebration of a reconquest without bloodshed."

She didn't answer for a moment, then she laughed softly. "So now I should call you 'Carlos the prophet.' Maybe you can tell me if we will have good rains next spring so that I can start preparing for long hours drying a bountiful crop of chili."

I laughed with her. "I'm afraid I can't tell you that, Sofía. The history of this time has a lot of holes in it, and there is also a lot I never learned."

Up ahead of us I saw Governor de Vargas disappear

from sight as he started down the steep bank of an arroyo. The company followed in a manner that reminded me of water falling over a spillway at the top of a dam. There was some confusion as the oxen tried to slow the heavy wagons pushing from behind, and then a lot of grunting and yells as the wagon drivers kept them moving across the arroyo bottom so they wouldn't stop and sink in the sand. Sofía and I joined the melee, hooting at the top of our lungs to help keep the caravan from stopping. By the time everyone had crossed the arroyo, Sofía and I were separated by several hundred yards.

I kneed Estrella gently, and in few minutes had rejoined Governor de Vargas at the head of the column. The governor and Lieutenant Montoya were deep in conversation and I rode silently alongside thinking about Sofía and her willingness to accept the story I told of my real life. Or, that is to say, my real life to come.

The trail now stretched over a long flat plain that allowed the wagons to proceed at a steady pace. By the time the sun came up, we were within sight of a massive black lava formation. Within an hour we had reached its base. The company stopped for a short rest, and the last of the water was poured into the troughs for the animals. I drank what remained of the stale water in my bag and looked ahead to where the trail ran next to the west side of the lava flow.

It was a desolate scene. The trail ran up the dry valley with mountains rising to the west. Stretching across the horizon to the east was a sea of black volcanic rock. Lieutenant Montoya called it *malpais*, or badlands. The only soil on it was that which the wind had blown into the cracks and dimples of the rock. There was almost no vegetation. Other than a few scrawny bushes that had managed to take hold in the nooks and crannies, it was completely lifeless. The small crevasses webbing the slick surface made it impassable on horseback, and the sharp, jagged stones looked like they would shred the leather of a man's boot before he could walk more than a few hundred yards.

Having studied maps of present day New Mexico at the library, I had a rough idea where we were. If I wasn't mistaken, the first ever atom bomb explosion had taken place not far from the eastern edge of the *malpais* at what would come to be called the Trinity Site. In a sort of weird way, it added new meaning to the name given this area by the Spaniards. It also crossed my mind that someone standing by these badlands some two hundred and fifty years from now would see an enormous flash of light and a rising mushroom cloud on the horizon. A few minutes later they would hear the thunder from an explosion that would forever change the course of human history. I guess I probably would have appreciated the moment a little more if I hadn't been so thirsty.

We were now feeling the full brunt of the sun. By noon we had managed to cover another ten miles. Usually Governor de Vargas would call for a halt so the caravan could take refuge from the afternoon heat. But today our march continued as the temperature easily passed the one hundred degree mark. I would have been happy to sip warm muddy water from an old boot.

An hour later the oxen were slowing down. They were struggling much more than usual with the burden of the wagons they were pulling. First one, and then another, let their tongues hang loose. Long thick ribbons of mucous dangled down, flapping like thin flags in the slow, hot breeze. I dropped back to the cattle being driven behind the company, and found them to be in the same condition. Their heads hung low and swayed from side to side, causing the mucous to form a bridge from their mouth to their chest.

The first animal to stop and lie down was a steer less than a year old. Its front legs buckled at the knees and its rump lowered slowly until it rested in the dirt. The whole company came to a halt and the Indians driving the cattle tried to make it stand up again. They yelled and whipped at its hind section with leather straps, but try as it might, the steer couldn't regain its feet. Governor de Vargas rode back and stood by as the Indians twisted its tail and kicked it in the ribs. Finally, at a signal from the governor, one of the Indians hit it on the head with the blunt side of an ax. The steer's eyes rolled back in its head. Another Indian jumped forward and grabbed the steer by its horns, quickly wrestling the head into position over a large stew pot that had been pulled from one of the wagons. A moment later one of the soldiers plunged a knife into the animal's throat and slit the arteries running through its neck. I turned my head aside and stared off into the horizon while its life's blood gushed out into the pot. When the bleeding, and the heart, had stopped, a group of soldiers tied a rope around the steer's hind legs and pulled it up into the back of a wagon. We couldn't take the time to field dress it properly so the carcass would have to be carried with us. Skinning and quartering would have to wait until we reached the Rio Grande, if and when we ever made it that far. As for the pot of blood, gruesome as it may sound, we lined up and took turns drinking a few swallows from a small cup. It wasn't quite as nasty as muddy water from a boot, but it was close.

Less than a mile later, one of the oxen stumbled and refused to get up. Its throat was slit, and the cargo in its wagon transferred to another cart. We continued to march—this time leaving the wagon and animal where it lay.

I knew the memory of those poor animals was going to haunt me for a long time to come. I had yelled at them like everyone else, trying to scare them back on their feet. I wanted to tell them that to stop meant death, but of course they would not have understood, so instead I stood by while they were killed. There wasn't any other choice. It was either continue forward, or lie down and wait for the end.

A little while later Sofía and I, more by circumstance than planning, found ourselves riding next to each other. Her cheeks had a layer of dust on them and her lips were swollen and cracked. But that didn't bother me nearly as much as the glazed look in her eyes. I wondered if I had the same look in mine.

We didn't talk much, and as we rode next to each other, the realization of our life and death struggle hit home. This is real life, Carlos, I said to myself. This isn't some horrid illusion out of Doctor Lopez's collection, but a real life nightmare where you may as easily die as live. Strange thoughts came to my mind. Maybe Dr. Lopez just wants to torture me, I thought. He's sitting in the comfort of his big house laughing at this little boy playing soldier. That is how he gets his jollies, I'll bet. But I'm not going to let him succeed. I'm going to make it through this dream, no matter what it takes.

It had to be the sun and heat that was making me think these crazy thoughts. Clear your mind, Carlos. You need to be strong. You need to continue the march, bring Sofía out of this and find Sage. That is what Doctor Lopez wants of me. I am here for a reason. I don't know what it is, but there is a reason.

I shook my head. I had to force myself back to the reality of the desert surrounding me. A deep fog seemed to lift itself from my brain. I looked over at Sofía and saw her swaying in the saddle. With a little pressure from my knee, Estrella moved closer until she was within a few inches of Sofía's horse. Sofía's chin had sunk to her chest and it looked as if she might topple from her horse. It was with a considerable effort that I reached out and touched her on the shoulder. My fingers grasped the rough cloth of her tunic and the thin arm beneath it. Her head came up and she turned toward me. After a moment, her eyes became the eyes that I had had gotten to know so well, and she smiled.

"Not to worry, Carlos. History says we are going to make it," she said in a raspy voice.

But I wasn't so sure. Perhaps we were an unwritten part of history. Maybe we were destined to die out here. But if that were to be, we would greet death with open eyes.

The wide valley had been shrinking as the contour of the lava flow pushed us closer to the foothills rising up to the mountains that flanked us on the west. Our path was littered with volcanic rocks and boulders that had, over the eons, broken off from the main body of lava. All around me I heard dull clunking sounds whenever the horses' hooves struck the black stones. The wagon wheels were taking a horrible beating as they rolled up and over the half-buried basalt. I had lost track of time and the sun seemed to have stopped moving. I was beginning to wonder if we were making any headway at all when a yell from Lieutenant Montoya rumbled out over the company.

I looked over in his direction and saw him pointing to a narrow pass in front of us. "Lava Gate!" he yelled, "We are at

Lava Gate!" The men stirred themselves from their daze and murmured to each other. I pushed Estrella forward and a few minutes later made my way through the narrow pass. Ahead the land opened up where the *malpais* ended. Far away in the distance, a thin band of green vegetation stretched northward until it disappeared over the horizon. I knew without being told that I was looking down into the Rio Grande Valley.

The soldiers spurred their horses forward but were brought up short by Lieutenant Montoya. We had been marching for almost twenty-four hours straight and still had several miles of desert to cross. To push our exhausted animals any faster would kill them. Instead, we continued our slow pace and watched as the cottonwoods along the valley began to take shape. Now the soldiers and wagon drivers struggled to rein in the animals. They too had seen the green of the valley and were trying to break into a run. By the time we reached the lush grass at the valley's edge, there was no controlling either man or beast. With many snorts, yells and whistles, the caravan rushed toward the water. Then we were pouring into the river. The animals waded in up to their chests and began taking long noisy swallows of water. The men dismounted, those with armor tossing it to the ground, and we all jumped in fully clothed.

There was singing and yelling, and a moment later I felt a pair of arms wrap around me from behind in a big hug. It was Sofía. I turned and returned the hug, and we both slipped and fell beneath the surface of the water. We came up coughing and laughing and then threw ourselves back into the water. Though she had shed her armor on the bank like the rest of the soldiers, she still wore the beanie like helmet strapped beneath her chin. A lock of her long, brown hair had come loose in the water. She stuffed it back under the helmet and I looked around to see if anyone had noticed. I needn't have worried; everyone was to busy enjoying the water.

Then I glanced behind me and saw Governor de Vargas floating on his back with his head raised like a polar bear at the zoo. His eye caught mine and he lifted one eyebrow before rolling over and disappearing under the water. A moment later he surfaced and paid no more attention to us.

9

Into Santa Fe

For three days we swam and ate and rested in the shadows of the cottonwoods at Fray Cristobal. The Indian wagon drivers spent their time repairing the damage to the carts caused by the *Jornada del Muerto* crossing. The soldiers welcomed the opportunity to care of the horses; replacing horseshoes that had been thrown or damaged. As for me, I kept busy mending saddles, bridles and leads. Somehow or another Sofía had been assigned to help. It was a good thing she was there. Though my skills working the leather had improved, they still weren't even close to her level of expertise.

Sofía had made the decision to reveal her identity after the crossing, but now that the time had come, she was having second thoughts.

"If I reveal myself, Carlos," she said one

afternoon while we patched a saddle with a broken stirrup, "the whole routine of the company will be changed. Now I am treated as a man. I am given no special consideration, and I ask for none. I think it best that the soldiers continue to see me as one of their own, at least for a little while longer."

She found a place along the river where the hanging branches of the bushes provided complete privacy. Finally she was able to bathe freely. Since the brutal crossing of the *Jornada,* she no longer seemed to notice the rigor and inconvenience of her metal armor and helmet.

"That's fine with me Sofía. If these men knew what they really had here, they would buzz around you like bees around a beautiful blossom," I said, feeling my cheeks heat up. She gave me a curious look and then smiled before turning back to the saddle.

"Thank you, Carlos," she said softly. "I think I shall take that as a compliment." I made myself busy with a rein that was coming loose from a bridle bit, and didn't say anything more.

Our peaceful rest along the river bank ended with the return of Captain del Charco and Lieutenant Campos. They rode into camp at full gallop and came to a stop in a dramatic flurry of dirt thrown up by their horses' hooves. I thought for a moment that there was a real urgency in their haste, but then decided it was nothing more than cheap theatrics.

After handing over the reins and giving unneeded instructions to a poor Indian driver who happened to be standing close, del Charco sauntered around the camp like a football jock in the school cafeteria. I happened to be sitting with Governor de Vargas and Lieutenant Montoya, and though no words were spoken between them, I couldn't help but notice the look of disdain they exchanged. Del Charco spent a few minutes slapping the soldiers on the back and talking in a loud voice that was guaranteed to make him the center of attention. Finally, he walked over to Governor de Vargas and greeted him.

"Governor, I am glad to see that you made the crossing of the *Jornada del Muerto* successfully. I must admit I had my doubts as to what I would find when I returned to Fray Cristobal."

"I'm sure you did, Captain," Governor de Vargas said dryly, "but as you have noted, the company came through superbly. I'm afraid I cannot take the credit for that, it was the men's high caliber that brought us this far."

Del Charco nodded in a short bow. "I'm sure the strength of the men is but a reflection of your leadership." Even when giving a compliment, I could hear the hidden sneer in del Charco's voice.

"Thank you, Captain. But tell me, what have you and the lieutenant learned. I have been anxiously awaiting your report."

"Yes, of course. It is not good, Governor. I am sorry to report that what we have seen does not bode well for the reconquest. We have ridden north as far as the Isleta and Sandia Pueblos. They are abandoned. We were puzzled by this, but a chance encounter along the trail provides some answers. Along the trail we came upon an Indian and his family. We talked to them at length, and learned that the inhabitants of the Pueblos know of your efforts and have fled to Santa Fe. Once there, they will band together and meet the company with a force of men intent on destroying each and every one of us."

"These are indeed bad tidings you bring, Captain," the governor said with a pained look on his face.

"I wish I was the bearer of more pleasant news, but what I tell you is the truth. You have often stated your desire to reclaim this land in a peaceful fashion, but I am afraid your wish has been thwarted by these heathen devils. There is but one option now. We must descend on Santa Fe with all the force we can muster. If we do so, without warning, we may be able to destroy their forces before they have a chance to resist."

I gave an involuntary start at the report del Charco was giving. This was not the history described to Sage and me by Doctor Lopez. What del Charco was talking about was nothing less than a wholesale massacre.

"Based upon what you say, Captain, it may be the only way to proceed. I must weigh your words carefully," Governor de Vargas said slowly.

Del Charco gave a snort of impatience. "You may weigh my words as you wish, Governor, but that will not change the facts I present to you. We must attack Santa Fe in force."

"As I said, Captain," Governor de Vargas replied sharply, "I will weigh your words carefully."

"Yes, Governor," del Charco said with small bow. "It is of course your decision on how we are to proceed."

"Yes, it is, Captain. But tell me, what about the family you learned this from?"

"The Indian family?"

"Yes, the Indian family."

"Having no further use for them, we left them where they were."

Governor de Vargas was quiet for a moment, studying the two men in front of him. Lieutenant Campos stared straight ahead like a statue carved from stone while del Charco smiled through thin bloodless lips.

"Very well, Captain. Both you and the lieutenant have traveled far. Rest yourself and your horses, for we will be leaving here tomorrow. The two of you will again ride ahead and see what further information you are able to gather."

"As you wish, Governor," del Charco replied with a nod of his head. Then they both turned and walked away. Governor de Vargas waited until they were out of hearing before he spoke.

"Is it just me, Lieutenant," he said, "or are you also wary of accepting del Charco's report at face value?"

"I think there is some truth in what he says, but I think you must look between his words to learn the entire truth. He will report whatever serves his own purpose, and nothing more nor less than that." I wasn't quite sure what Lieutenant Montoya meant, but the governor nodded in silent agreement.

Del Charco and Campos rode north up the river valley early the next morning. It was almost noon before the company had finished loading the wagons and saddling the horses. When everything was ready, we continued our march north. The sun was as harsh as it had been during the crossing of the *Jornada*, but the animals and men were well rested and water was now plentiful. Compared to the ordeal of our desert crossing, the afternoon trek was almost like a nature walk on a school field trip.

We had been moving at a good pace for several hours when Lieutenant Montoya spotted several large black birds circling a few miles to the northeast. From the way they were flying, he thought them to be turkey vultures hovering over a dead or dying animal. Governor de Vargas decided to investigate. Sofía and I were riding near the head of the column of soldiers and wagons when he called me over.

"Carlos, go and see what those birds have found," he said. "It is probably nothing of any consequence, but we had better make sure."

"Take a soldier with you," added Lieutenant Montoya. "I don't think there will be any danger, but it is well to have someone watch to the back while you watch to the front."

"Yes, sir," I replied, giving a tug at Estrella's reins and trotting back to Sofía.

"C'mon," I said when I got close. "We have been assigned to see what has caught those birds' attention." Sofía wrinkled her nose and an expression of repugnance crossed her face.

"I have no desire to see the rotting corpse of a deer or badger, Carlos," she said.

"It is a dirty job, sister, but someone has got to do it," I replied in my best imitation of John Wayne. She gave me a puzzled look.

"Why are you talking funny?"

"Never mind," I sighed. "Just a joke from my past and your future."

"Honestly, Carlos, sometimes I think you really are crazy." But she turned her horse and we began to make our way across the plain toward the circling birds. With a light kick of our heels, the horses broke into a trot. Within a few minutes the company disappeared from view as we crossed over a low rolling hill.

It was nice to get away for a while. I guess in some ways I'm a loner. I liked the stories the men told and the songs they sang, but this was the first time in several weeks that I was free from the constant sounds of the rolling wagons, thudding hooves and squeaking saddles—not to mention the ever present cloud of dust thrown up in the air by our passing.

Up ahead, probably about a half-mile in the distance, the flat plain was broken by a narrow arroyo. It seemed to be the focal point for the hovering birds, and we headed in that direction. As we got closer, I could see that the banks were steep, almost like the banks of a canyon. The faint odor of rotting meat hit my nose, and a moment later I heard the buzzing of flies and, more ominous, low growling sounds.

"Maybe you better wait here," I said uneasily. "It's probably not going to be pretty."

In reply, Sofía shot me a withering look. With a sharp kick to her horse's flanks, she sped ahead and reached the edge of the arroyo a few seconds ahead of me. Looking over the edge, her jaw clamped shut so hard I could see the muscles tighten in her face. A small noise escaped her clenched lips and she did a quick sign of the cross. I pulled Estrella up beside her and looked down at the ghastly sight below.

There were four of them. It took me a moment to sort through the mangled mess, but it looked like a woman, a man and two children. Four coyotes were so busy eyeing each other over the decomposing bodies that they didn't even look up. A few feet away several of the black birds were hopping about, trying to grab chunks of flesh without being bitten by the coyotes.

"Hyaah, get out of here!" I yelled.

The coyotes jumped back in surprise and stood looking up at us. I yelled again and they slowly turned and trotted away with wicked-looking backward glances. The birds flapped their wings a few times, and then started to move in on the bodies.

I spotted a break in the bank of the arroyo about a hundred yards down and moved Estrella toward it. Sofía followed silently. Once on the sandy bottom, we backtracked to our grisly find. As we got closer, the horses balked and tried to turn away. After a few more steps we had to dismount and proceed on foot. The horses were well trained and stood where we left them, though they shuffled nervously and made loud windy noises as they blew air through their nostrils.

I asked Sofía, in what I hoped was a steady voice, if she wanted to stay behind while I got a closer look at the bodies. She shook her head, but didn't say anything. I shrugged my shoulders and we moved forward.

The birds flew off with a loud clatter of wings as we approached. For a moment we stood looking down at the remains. The coyotes had done quite a job on them, but I could still tell from the tattered clothes that they were Indians. Sofía silently pointed to the man's fingers. Some were bent backwards in an unnatural angle, and two others severed completely from the hand.

"Del Charco," she whispered, almost as if to herself.

"You think these are the Indians he said he questioned?" I asked in horror.

"Questioned? He didn't question them. He tortured them. Look at their ankles," she said grimly, pointing to their feet. I hadn't noticed before, but all four had thin strands of leather tied about their ankles. The arms of the woman and children were hidden behind their back. Holding my breath, I reached down and turned one of the children over. Their hands had been bound behind them. Looking closer at the woman and children's necks, between the spots where the coyotes had gnawed, I saw deep slashes that could only have been made with a sharp knife. Their blood had blackened the sand beneath them. The man had taken a huge blow to the head that had caved his skull in above his right ear.

Through the stench, I forced myself to take a deep breath. "C'mon. We need to tell the governor about this…this mess." Sofía nodded and we hurried back to our horses. Once out of the arroyo, we kicked our horses into a gallop and a few minutes later rejoined the company. Governor de Vargas had seen us coming, and had brought the caravan to a stop by the time we reached him.

Sofía disappeared into the line of soldiers while I told him of our find. He sat motionless with a dark expression on his face as I described what we had found. I didn't mention del Charco, but when I finished he turned his head toward Lieutenant Montoya.

"Well, he said he left them where they were," he murmured. "He just didn't say in what condition." Lieutenant Montoya shook his head and curled his lip in disgust. "Take a couple of soldiers and some shovels," Governor de Vargas ordered, speaking to me, "and attend to the bodies. Let Father Chavez know. He'll want to give them a proper burial. I'll hold the company here until you get back."

It took us about three hours to finish our morbid task. We dug a deep hole and laid the parents in the middle with one child on each side. I had to bite my lip when we tossed the dirt onto the bodies. The thump of the shovel's load of dirt landing on their bodies made me cringe inside. I kept telling myself that back in my real world they had long since turned to dust.

The governor didn't waste any time once we got back, and a short time later the march resumed. By nightfall the grave was far behind, but the smell of the bodies seemed to linger in the air.

We marched without any serious interruptions for a few days. As we moved further north I began to notice small changes in the terrain. It was still a far cry from what anyone could call a lush environment, but the grass grew thicker and we saw more wildlife in the form of small coveys of quail and little groups of deer that bolted as we got close.

Two days later mud houses appeared on the horizon. It was the Pueblo of Isleta. The soldiers held their spears tighter as we got close, but the Pueblo, as had been reported by del Charco, was abandoned. The sign of human activity was easy to see—fire pits with recently burned wood and still moist squash drying on racks in the sun—but if there were Indians around, they were well hidden. A large church, centered among the squat adobe structures, dominated the plaza. Inside, it was in dust-covered shambles. The pews were all gone, probably used for firewood, and the altar had been burned. Brass candleholders lay on the floor where they had come to rest during the Pueblo Revolt twelve years earlier.

We continued our march, and later that day passed through Sandia Pueblo. It too had been abandoned.

That night we camped on the broad plain leading up to the Sandia Mountains in roughly the same place where Coronado had camped during the first European exploration of the southwest a hundred and fifty years earlier. If I remembered my history lessons correctly, he had taken their food by force in the middle of winter for his own men. The Indians had had to escape by fleeing into the river's frigid waters. Looking across the wide river, I shuddered thinking of the women, children and men who had probably not made it to the other side, or had frozen or starved to death afterward.

Not exactly a shining moment in American history.

The next day we continued our march up the Rio Grande valley, passing the pueblos of Santa Ana, San Felipe and Santo Domingo. All were abandoned. The deserted pueblos were worrying the governor. It seemed that del Charco had at least been truthful in one respect. The Indians were leaving the pueblos as we got close.

Speaking of the Devil, shortly after leaving Santo Domingo Pueblo we were rejoined by del Charco and Lieutenant Campos at the base of a steep volcanic shelf that Lieutenant Montoya called *La Bajada*, "The Drop," in English. But from where we stood it wasn't a drop, but a long, steep rise formed during an ancient eruption of a solitary mountain a few miles to the north of us. The road, if you could call it that, was a set of almost invisible twin ruts that snaked their way up to the top through a series of switchbacks. Even with the switchbacks, I didn't think the distance to reach the top was more than two miles. As such, I was a little surprised when the governor, with several hours of light remaining, ordered a halt for the day.

The reason for the early stop became apparent the next morning. Though we started early, it wasn't until late in the afternoon that the whole company had finally struggled to the top of the plateau. It wasn't too bad for the livestock or horses carrying riders. Mostly they let the animals pick their way slowly among the rocks and boulders. It was the wagons that slowed us down. No matter how hard the oxen and horses pulled, the wagons seemed to roll back two feet for every foot they moved forward. Finally the governor ordered the horsemen to ride their mounts to the top, walk back down, and then help push the wagons from behind. My job was to walk next to one of the wagons with a thick chunk of wood that could be thrown behind the wheels when it began to slide backward. Sofía had the same task behind me on another wagon. It was easier than pushing from behind, but I had to move fast and take care that my hand didn't get caught between the wood and the wheel. I wished Sofía had been assigned to push a wagon from behind, even if it was harder work. The thought of her delicate hand crushed beneath the weight of the wagon played in my mind. But I needn't have worried; all the wagons finally made it without any mangled limbs—just a few splinters that could be plucked out later.

The black volcanic rocks alongside the road were tattooed with petroglyphs—ancient Indian images of stick men, animals and strange looking circles. Amid them, and obviously of more recent times, were crosses chiseled by Spaniards traveling the road. I guessed the crosses were supposed to scare away any of the Indian gods hanging around. Or maybe it was like gangs marking their territory with graffiti.

Once the last wagon reached the top, we stopped to rest. Behind us to the south were the beautiful blues, greens and red of the Rio Grande Valley. To the north and east was a gently sloping plain—thick with gramma grass and juniper trees—that descended to the foothills of the Sangre de Christo Mountains ten miles away. And there, just barely visible to the eye, was Santa Fe.

We marched for another three or four miles, making camp close to where the Cochiti Trail between Santo Domingo and Santa Fe intersected with the San Ildefonso Trail, which Lieutenant Montoya said was the primary trail leading to the northern pueblos. A scout reported back that the trails were empty but showed recent signs of considerable foot and horse traffic into Santa Fe.

After making camp I sat resting in the shade of the wagons. Sofía had joined me, but we didn't speak much; our attention was focused on the governor and del Charco. The two were walking out in the gramma grass by themselves. We couldn't hear what was said, but from their animated movements it was obviously a heated discussion. Suddenly they stopped walking and del Charco came to rigid attention— staring straight ahead without speaking. The governor's face was no more than a few inches from his and we could now hear him as the level of his voice rose, but the words were unintelligible. Then there was a moment of silence and it seemed they were locked in an invisible struggle. Abruptly del Charco's hand came up in a formal salute and he pivoted and walked away to the edge of the main company where Lieutenant Campos sat silently by himself. The governor stared at his retreating back for a few seconds before turning and heading back to the camp.

"Is everything all right, Governor?" I asked as he passed by. For a moment I didn't think he had heard me. Then he stopped and stared at me. His face was masked with controlled fury unlike any I had ever seen.

"What? What is that you said?" he asked in an angry voice, and though he was looking straight at us, I got the feeling that he wasn't really seeing us. His anger had silenced me and I couldn't answer. Suddenly the lines on his face softened and his eyes were focused again. He forced himself to swallow, and then he spoke in an even voice.

"No, Carlos, everything is not alright. It appears that the Pueblo Indians are gathering en mass at Santa Fe. I have hoped for a peaceful entry into the city, but del Charco advises me that such an approach would be foolhardy. As usual, he counsels that force is the only alternative we have, and the facts he presents make a convincing argument. I fear that an example may be needed to show the Pueblos that resistance to our presence will be costly."

A hollow feeling filled my stomach, and it was my turn to swallow before speaking. "What...what do you mean?" I asked, even though I had a pretty good idea what the answer would be.

"I will have no choice but to attack with all the force we can muster. And when we are victorious—which I have no doubt we will be—I will again have no choice but to extract a terrible punishment for their opposition. An example must be made that will ensure a halt to any thoughts of resistance from the Indians. Once we have taken Santa Fe, I will order the execution of those who have raised arms against us." His voice trailed away into a whisper as he spoke and horror gripped me as I listened to his words.

"You can't do that!" I said sharply. "You said you wanted history to remember you as a leader, not a butcher. If you start executing the Indians, you will be no different than del Charco." The governor's face flushed red and sparks of anger were rekindled in his eyes. Sofía shot me an alarmed look. She shook her head back and forth slightly, signaling me to quit this dangerous talk before I roused his anger even further. But I knew it was del Charco speaking through him, and I wasn't about to be silenced.

"This was these people's world for centuries before we came here. They did not invite us any more than the English were invited onto this continent's eastern shore. But that is the way of the world—great empires are busily claiming their parts of this new land. There will be dozens, if not hundreds, of conquests. You have the opportunity to set this one apart from all the others.

"Governor, the other conquests will not be celebrated. In fact, they will probably be reviled because of the atrocities committed in the pursuit of victory. But this campaign can be remembered in history as one of the few times that peace was brought without death and punishment to those that will be part of the Empire."

The anger drained from his face, and he stared at me with a curious expression. I think he was going to say something, but before he could speak I pressed on. "There may be no choice but to battle the Pueblo Indians, but before that happens, I think you should make every effort possible to fulfill your orders without bloodshed. That is what you have intended all along. Don't let the likes of del Charco change the course that you yourself know is right."

They were both silent waiting for me to continue, but I didn't know what else to say.

Sofía's expression had turned from alarm to pride as I spoke. There was a sparkle in her eyes that I pretended not to notice.

"There is wisdom in your words, Carlos. Your capacity to provide counsel was unknown to me before now. I will consider what you have said." He looked to Sofía, and then back to me.

"Rest now," he said, turning away slowly, "we will enter Santa Fe before sunrise tomorrow morning."

10

Sage, the Owl and the Arrival of the Metal People

Images of my Dream Brother, Carlos, continued to visit me in my sleep, and each morning Lonewolf and Wise Father gently questioned me about my nighttime visions. I told them what I could. Wise Father betrayed no emotion, but listened carefully. Lonewolf, though, became increasingly agitated and I would see him walking up and down the river bank in deep thought after we had talked. After one night of dreams—dreams in which Carlos left the dry dust of the desert and swam in the Great River—Lonewolf rode south with four other men of the Pueblo. Nothing was said to me about his departure, but I knew he was searching for signs of those I saw in my dreams.

The morning they left, I found myself walking through the plaza and watching the activity around me. I didn't stop to talk or play; I felt the need to be alone with my thoughts. Stone danced about with the children clinging to his back and shoulders. Blue Medicine Flower had wrapped her arms around his thick thigh and made a pedestal of his foot. She squealed with joy, yelling at him to move faster and faster. I smiled at their antics, but found myself distanced from the other children—not by anything they did, but by my own distraction. Something was different. Something was happening to me. I had tried to run and play during the past several days, and then would stop in mid-step as thoughts I did not understand forced themselves into my consciousness. It was small things that triggered thoughts of a different place. The sounds of the noisy games brought forth images of an open space surrounding a building where lessons were taught. In the open space children swung on seats tied with metal cords to angled poles buried in the ground. Their style of dress was unlike any I had seen, but, for some reason, it was not unfamiliar to me.

I paused and watched the women laughing and talking next to the *hornos* as they waited for the day's bread to finish baking. I closed my eyes, and suddenly, in my mind, the *horno* was a white square chest, hot from an invisible fire within. A hinged door was mounted on its front. Standing in front of the chest, stirring a pot resting above a fire that breathed from its top, a young woman with her head slightly tipped forward concentrated on the markings of a box in her hand. Then she looked up. A tight smile of resignation was upon her lips and her dark eyes were staring directly at me. I gave an involuntary gasp and heard a small moan come from my throat. There was no doubt as to who I was seeing.

She was my mother—but not the mother I knew. She

was not the mother who had played with me in the waters of the river and under the summer leaves of the fruit trees. She was not the mother I remembered withering away from a sickness within her chest that first took her breath, and, finally, her spirit.

"What is the matter, Sage? Why does your body shake?" Wise Father asked from behind me. I had not heard him join me and gave a little start as his words broke the stream of my thoughts. My eyes opened and the vision was gone. The plaza was as it had always been.

"I saw my mother, Wise Father," I said in a low, trembling voice.

"You saw Golden Leaf?" he asked, his voice jumping in excitement. Golden Leaf had been his youngest, and, I think, his favorite daughter.

"No, Wise Father," I said, hating to disappoint him, "it was a mother I have no memory of, but who is as real as Golden Leaf." I felt a burning in my eyes and a tear rolled down my cheek. Wise Father put his hands on my shoulders and turned me gently until I was staring into his lined and weathered face.

"Is she also your Dream Brother's mother?" he asked

"Yes, I think she is," I said with my voice breaking, "and I miss her as much as I do Golden Leaf." I gave a small sob and tears came freely. Wise Father took me in his arms and I buried my face in his chest.

"Oh, Wise Father, what is this about? Why are these thoughts filling my head?"

"I don't know, Sage," he said uncertainly. The sounds of the children playing subsided and I could feel them looking over at us. Wise Father also noticed their sudden attention. "I do not wish to alarm the smaller children with your tears. Join me in a walk along the river. I have found that the sound of the water passing over the rocks can be very soothing." I nodded and wiped at my tears with the back of my hand. After a few deep breaths I felt the lump in my throat grow smaller.

We turned and moved south toward the river. Not far from the plaza, Wise Father greeted two women working in a place we called the flat, windy spot. It was an area where no trees or hills blocked the breeze that usually blew from the south in the morning hours. In the women's hands were large, shallow baskets filled with growths of wheat that had been pulverized under the oxen's hooves. I watched as they tossed the crushed stalks into the air with one swooping motion. The steady breeze caught the chaff in its downward fall and pushed it out of the flat, windy spot before it reached the ground. The heavier grains fell to the hard packed dirt and would later be collected and ground into flour for the bread.

Once past the women, we were walking through fields of corn and squash. It had been a good summer with plentiful rains. Most of the men and older boys were busy clearing weeds growing in the small channels that delivered water from the river. Others were searching through the squash for those that had come of size. The corn would remain on the tall stalks until past the first frost. Then it would be harvested, dried and added to the winter storage, which still held many kernels from the previous year's growing season. When the rains were sparse, the Pueblo would be secure with enough stored food for several winters.

At the time of planting, the whole Pueblo had come out to the fresh furrows of rich brown earth and Wise Father, as the *chielo* of the summer season, had performed the ceremony necessary so as to not offend the spirits of the Water People from which all water came. Later in the year, when the cold months arrived and nothing would grow, the Pueblo would spend the days hunting for meat. At that time, the winter *chielo* would take over the leadership of the Pueblo from Wise Father and perform a similar ceremony, helping to insure that wild game was plentiful.

Within a few minutes we had left the fields and were at the riverbank. This late in the summer, the sometimes torrential river was no more than a small stream. The trees that spread their branches over its banks shielded us from the sun. A small path ran alongside the water and we walked upstream without talking. Wise Father moved as one who was much younger than the years his body showed, and before long we were making our way up the river into a mountain valley. As we climbed higher, the leafy trees disappeared— replaced by tall pines and a dense tangle of brush. Alongside the path white flowers were blooming among long green grass that had gone to seed.

I was breathing hard and Wise Father slowed his step as I started to fall behind. Shortly we stopped and rested on a large rock jutting out over the clear, cold water of the river. The fresh smell of the forest and the gurgling of the river brought a peaceful feeling to me, and my visions and dreams weighed less upon me.

"I notice you no longer play in the games of the other children, Sage," Wise Father said with a questioning tone in his voice.

"I have no desire to play," I replied evenly.

"Is it because of the dreams?"

I nodded slowly. "That is part of it, Wise Father. That

and the worry they bring out in Lonewolf and the others of the Pueblo. The dreams come unbidden, but I sometimes fear that Lonewolf is angry at me for what I cannot control."

Wise Father smiled and put his thin arm around me. His hand gripped my shoulder tightly for a moment before he spoke. "No, no Sage. You must never think that he, or any others of the Pueblo, are angry at you. He fears the tidings you bring, but he, as do I, welcome the gift that comes to us from you. It is unfortunate that one so young must carry concerns that should be reserved for those who have more years than you."

"I am not so young, Wise Father. I have seen fourteen summers and have completed the Finishing Ceremony," I reminded him.

"Yes, but only two moons have passed since then."

"Does not the Finishing Ceremony mean I have passed into womanhood?"

Wise Father did not answer immediately and sat staring at the water in silent thought. While I waited for his response, I thought back to the Finishing Ceremony. On that night I had bathed and gone to bed as usual. I had not been asleep long when I was awakened by one of the women of the Pueblo. She gave me a long black wool dress to wear, but would not answer any of my questions. Instead she led me to the *kiva* of the summer people and left me with several other of my friends who had also been gathered there.

We huddled together, both frightened and curious. The entrance to the *kiva*, on its roof, opened in front of us, and we waited anxiously until we were joined by one of the men of the Pueblo. He beckoned to us and we followed him down the ladder rising from below through the top of the *kiva*. I looked through the opening anxiously—it was a place that only the men could go—and climbed down quickly. For a moment I felt as if I had climbed down into a giant *horno*. The walls made a domed circle around us with the entrance high above. A wooden seat ran along the perimeter of the *kiva*. Built into one wall was a small fire pit. The girls were separated from the boys, and we moved into a small room adjacent to the main *kiva*. Then we stood, quietly waiting.

I gave a start when loud footsteps reverberated through the room from something moving heavily about on the roof above us. Two of the Pueblo men held up a blanket, blocking our view of the entrance. Suddenly they pulled the blanket aside and we huddled closer together at the sight of a figure dressed in deerskins and wearing a painted mask. One of the men addressed him, calling him a god from the place where our people had been born. He then spoke to the masked creature, telling him he had been called from his home beneath the lake to bring the girls to womanhood. We were then lined up and told to raise our arms. The god was handed a blade from a yucca cactus and he stepped behind us with his arm poised to strike with the long green frond. I closed my eyes and waited for the sting of the yucca, but as the shiny leaf was brought down in a swinging arc, the god's hand slowed and I felt only its light touch on either side of my body. His movements were repeated for each of the young girls. We were led up the ladder and returned to our rooms. The Finishing Ceremony was complete. We had been brought into womanhood.

The next day I saw the boys, some of whom were shirtless. Their rib cages were covered in fiery red welts. We asked them what happened, but they refused to answer. Finally I was able to get one of my best friends, Cactus, to reluctantly tell me parts of what had happened after the girls had been returned to their beds. The welts were from the same god who had appeared before me, he said. Like the young women, the boys were lined up facing in the same direction and instructed to raise their arms. Unlike us, the god had swung the cactus through the air in a hissing arc that crossed their ribs. Several of the young men had had their skin actually laid open from the blow inflicted with the yucca. Afterward, the god removed his mask, and the young men found themselves staring into the smiling face of one of the men of the Pueblo. When their surprise had gone, they each took turns wearing the mask. During the imitation, the men and boys laughed and joked among themselves. Later, other masks were brought from a hidden area in the *kiva* and the boys were instructed on the ways of imitating each of the other gods in preparation for the ceremony of their coming. As Cactus told me the story, I looked at the angry welts across his ribs and was thankful that the Finishing Ceremony for girls was so less painful.

Wise Father gave a small sigh. "You are right, Sage. But your womanhood is still new, and it would have been better if more time passed before these dreams were sent to you." He shrugged his shoulders in resignation and continued. "It may also be that I am reluctant to let your being as a small girl fade into memory. Soon you will join with a male of the Pueblo and begin to have children of your own. I will be very lonely then, but that is the way..."

I quickly looked over to Wise Father as he stopped talking in mid-sentence. His eyes were fixed on a tree across the river from us. "What is it, Wise Father?" I asked.

He lifted his hand and pointed to the tree. There, in a bare spot on a lone branch, I saw what had caught his

169

attention. It was a large owl, the biggest I had ever seen, and it was gazing at us with unblinking yellow eyes. Wise Father rose slowly to his feet. I too started to rise, but he held up his hand and gestured for me to remain seated. Still staring at the owl, he walked backward several paces down the riverbank. The owl didn't seem to notice and kept its eyes fixed on me. Wise Father walked back and rejoined me with a curious expression on his face.

"What is it, Wise Father?"

"I am not sure, Sage," he murmured. "Look how he stares at you."

Suddenly the owl cocked it furry head to one side and fixed its gaze at a point on the path where it curved around a rock and disappeared up the valley. Abruptly the owl dropped from its perch and its huge wings spread wide. It seemed to be heading directly for us, but instead passed several feet above our heads. There was a brief whisper of the wind as its outstretched wings sliced the air, and then it disappeared into the forest behind us. I opened my mouth to speak, but Wise Father silenced me with a sign from his outstretched hand.

"Follow me," he whispered urgently. I rose quickly from my seat on the rock and followed him as he moved swiftly into a thicket of brush alongside the path. Once there he lowered himself into a prone position and signaled me to join him. I had done no more than lay upon the ground when I heard the thump of horses hooves muffled by the fallen pine needles. Around the curve in the path rode three men on horseback. Their long black hair hung free to their shoulders and they wore leggings of the Comanche. They crossed slowly in front of our hiding place—so close that I could smell the sweat that matted the horses' chests. As they passed, I saw first one and then the other horses' ears prick up and their nostrils flare as they detected our smell. The Comanches' caught the change in the animal's behavior and the front rider brought them to a stop. My heart was pounding in my chest and I held my breath as they peered into the brush around them. I knew that it was only a matter of seconds before they would find us. I also knew the Comanche way would be to kill Wise Father and take me back to their people as a prisoner. Wise Father turned his head slowly until his lips were next to my ear.

"Run when I attack," he whispered in a voice so soft that I felt, rather than heard, his words. His body tensed up next to mine as he prepared to send his old body into its death fight. But I knew I couldn't run and leave him to fight against the three younger and stronger men. Instead my eyes desperately searched the areas around me for a rock or club that would serve as a weapon. Then, before either of us could move, the wind whispered and a long, high shriek tore through the air from above us. It was a horrible sound that sent a shiver through my body, and it was with only a mighty effort that I kept from raising my hands to cover my ears.

The reaction of the horses was instantaneous and powerful. With an explosion of hooves they broke into a full gallop down the path upon which we had been walking. The Comanches were taken by surprise, and only through superb riding were they able to cling to the backs of the frightened animals. I watched through the leaves as they finally reined their horses to a halt about a hundred paces from where we lay. They spoke softly to the horses and managed to turn them back in our direction.

Then the loud screech was repeated, and the longhaired riders struggled anew with their mounts as they turned in circles and moved violently from side to side. When they had regained control, a hurried conversation could be seen taking place, which was followed by nervous laughter when one of the men pointed to the top of the tree next to where we lay. A moment later they were riding away from us and quickly disappeared from sight around another curve in the path.

As one, Wise Father and I rose to our feet and moved as rapidly as possible away from the path and into the cover of the forest. Once we had put a safe distance between ourselves and the river, Wise Father paused so we could catch our breath.

"I think we are safe for now," he said, gasping for air as he spoke, "but it is best if we stay away from the trail. They may double back, and I think one encounter is enough for today."

"One encounter is enough forever," I said, picking at the twigs and grass that clung to my hair. "I was sure that that was the end of our time in this world. We were lucky the owl chose that moment to give his call."

Wise Father looked over at me and a puzzled look crossed his wrinkled brow. "Do you think it was a matter of chance that your owl happened to be there?"

"My owl? What do you mean, Wise Father?"

"Look behind you," he said, staring over my shoulder. "He has stayed with us." I whirled around. A short way from where we stood, the gray bird perched on the branch of a tree. He sat unmoving, staring over our heads into the woods. I walked slowly toward him until I was almost directly below the branch on which he rested. He looked down for a moment, and then began preening the soft, downy feathers on his chest, giving me no more attention. Wise Father walked over to me, but the owl continued to ignore both of us. Wise Father was still breathing hard, and he lay his hand on my shoulder for support.

"Are you all right?" I asked as I felt him totter.

"I am fine, Sage. The days when this old body could run through the woods like a young warrior have long since passed. We will walk slowly back to the Pueblo so I may regain my energy. But we should start immediately and give warning that Comanche scouts are close by."

"Do you think they will attack the Pueblo?"

"No, they will stay hidden and watch from afar," he said with a look upon his face as if he had bitten into a bad tasting fruit. "Then, after they have studied us, they will return to their people and plan a raid upon our horses or stockpiles of food."

Raiding bands of Comanche, Ute and Apache had become more and more commonplace over the past several years. Sometimes they would come in the night and the Pueblo would awaken in the morning to find our horses and livestock gone. Other times, when their numbers were large, they would ride from the hills with frightful yells and screams, and take whatever they could before the men of the Pueblo engaged them in battle. Oftentimes, one or more of our people would fall from the arrow or lance.

Wise Father and I walked through the trees back toward the Pueblo. The gray owl followed quietly behind us. At times he would swoop low and disappear into the forest in front of us. Then the trees thinned and soon we were walking across the fields. As we moved toward the mud buildings, the owl passed over our heads one last time, and then turned and disappeared into the woods with a strong, graceful flap of his wings.

A large number of people were now gathered in the plaza, many strangers to me. Some spoke in the familiar tongue of our *Tewa* language, but there were also many conversing with words I could not understand. Most had ponies weighed down with blankets and baskets of food. The children of the strangers huddled with eyes wide, clinging to the skirts of the women, while the men grouped together and talked about matters that, judging from the tight expressions on their faces, were of the utmost seriousness. I stayed close to Wise Father as he moved toward them. When they saw him coming, the talking ceased and one of the warriors who had ridden south with Lonewolf broke from the group and hurried to greet us. It was Willow, a young man of no more than twenty summers. He smelled of sweat, and the dust from his travel hung in his hair and clothes.

"Wise Father," he said in a voice choked with excitement and relief, "we have been searching for you. I was beginning to fear you would not return."

"Lose your fear, Willow, I am here," Wise Father said sternly. "Tell me quickly what causes you to behave as an old woman. What has happened to Lonewolf? Why is he not with you?" Willow took a deep breath and, with a visible effort, brought his excitement under control.

"Lonewolf is well. He has sent me to bring you the news of what we have learned."

"And what is that?" Wise Father asked in a gentler voice.

"A group of the Metal People are marching up the Big River toward Santa Fe," Willow exclaimed. Wise Father nodded but didn't show any sign of surprise. His demeanor seemed to soothe the young man and he continued speaking.

"After leaving here, we rode south until we reached Isleta. There we found the people of the village preparing to flee to the mountains and hide from the Metal People. Lonewolf urged them instead to come here. The ones you see,"

 174

he said pointing to the people crowding the plaza, "are those that heeded his advice. Many others felt that coming to Santa Fe was the same as coming to fight the Metal People, and they continued their flight into the hills. I was sent to guide these ones here. Lonewolf rides a day behind me. He is stopping at the other villages to warn and advise them. But there are also many I met on the trail who have followed me here."

"How far behind you are the Metal People?" Wise Father asked.

"I think several days. They have stopped to rest after completing the long march across the desert."

"How do you know this?"

"They were watched by a scout from Isleta."

"And how long has it been since the scout saw them?"

Willow counted back the days in his head and took a few seconds to answer. "At least three or four sunrises have passed since they were seen."

Wise Father considered Willow's words before speaking. "In that many days, the Metal People could have traveled far. But Lonewolf would have made his way here immediately if they were close. I think they must still be at least two days from here.

"Willow, bring the women together and let us see if we can make room for the beds of the strangers." The young man nodded and hurried off. Wise Father moved across the plaza toward the group of men, and I walked close by his side.

"That was not very nice, Wise Father," I said.

Wise Father stopped in surprise and stared at me. "What was not nice, Sage?"

"Telling Willow that his behavior was like that of an old woman. The women of the Pueblo would not be pleased to hear of your comparison."

"Hmm. As usual, you are right Sage. Next time I will take more care in the choice of my words. Uh...you won't... uh..."

"I shall not say another word about this, Wise Father." His lined face broke into a crinkled grin.

"Thank you, Sage. The last thing I need is for Dear Dancer to rebuke me for an unintended slight. We played together as children and I would rather face a mother bear than incur her anger." He gave a snort and we laughed together before he went to greet the strangers.

I went off to find Willow and help with the children. As I crossed the plaza, I heard Stone laughing. He was sitting with his back against the pueblo wall playing with a small brown puppy that pulled and growled at a scrap of leather held in his hand. I paused to watch them at play. Stone seemed oblivious to the people that filled the plaza. At times I would feel sad for Stone—a full-grown man with the mind of a small child. But now, looking at him as he scratched behind the puppy's ears, I envied him. He had no worries or cares. The approaching Spaniards and raiding Comanche were of no concern. He played all day and slept soundly at night. I didn't think his mind could ever be consumed with the complex thoughts of dream brothers and alien worlds. I walked over to him and bent down to pet the wriggling puppy, which immediately forgot about the leather toy and started nipping at my fingers.

"Doenee," Stone said.

"Doenee," I repeated. "Is that the name of your new puppy?" Stone nodded quickly.

"That is a nice name," I said. I had not seen the puppy before and decided that it must have come with one of the newly arrived families. "Hello, Doenee." The little dog rolled over on his back and I stroked his chest. Its dark eyes stared straight up into the sky and one of its tiny hind legs scratched furiously at nothing in the air above it.

"Oooh," I said with a high-pitched squeal, "he is so cute." I rubbed his chest a few more times and then stood up to leave. Doenee continued to lie on his back and looked up at me with an expectant stare, as if asking why I was stopping now. I bent down and picked up the puppy and lay him in Stone's lap.

"I have to go help now, but I'll come visit you later," I said. Stone nodded once and shook the piece of leather in front of Doenee's nose, forgetting about me as their play continued.

The rest of the day passed swiftly as I helped take care of the children and prepare their food. The approaching soldiers were like a storm cloud hanging above us, but even so, there was an atmosphere like those that surrounded our celebrations. The children were soon yelling and running and jumping together, even though many of them spoke different languages. Several of the women from the different Pueblos knew each other from years passed, and there was a renewing of old acquaintances. Dinner was eaten late that evening and I had to fight to stay awake. The walk through the woods, the encounter with the Comanche and the work accommodating the visitors had drained me of my energy. After dinner, I went back to my bed, crawling over several deerskins that had been placed in my room for the children of the other Pueblos. I fell into a deep sleep with no dreams to wake me. I don't remember hearing the other children go to bed, but in the morning sleeping bodies surrounded me.

People from the other Pueblos continued to arrive

throughout the following day. With each new group, Wise Father would hurry from his seat in the shade to learn what news they brought about the Metal People and Lonewolf. Then he would return to sit in quiet contemplation. The men continued to group together and discuss the meaning of each new bit of information, but they kept a respectful distance from Wise Father. They all knew, as did I, that he was anxious to confer with Lonewolf. Plans and strategies were needed, and the advice of his War Chief was crucial.

Finally, late in the afternoon, Lonewolf rode into the plaza with a large band of warriors. Now was the time for decisions. The spiritual leaders of the many villages joined Wise Father and Lonewolf and went solemnly to the *kiva*, disappearing through the opening in the roof. Females were not allowed into the *kiva*, but Cactus went in with the men. He would not participate in the discussions, but would carry out any minor errands that might arise. I was anxious to learn of their words, and when the men emerged a few hours later, I cornered Cactus and, with a little urging, made him tell me what had passed.

His story was brief. Wise Father had formally welcomed the other leaders and prayers had been offered up to the Gods under the lake. Lonewolf had then told of his findings during the days since he had sent Willow back to our Village. Most of his time had been spent trying to convince the Indians in the southern Pueblos to make the journey to Santa Fe and join forces to oppose the oncoming Metal People. When the Metal People were spotted at *Kewa*, what the Metal People called Santo Domingo, the Indians had hurriedly ridden to our Pueblo in Santa Fe.

When Lonewolf finished his account of what had

happened, the talk turned to how the Pueblos should respond to the threat posed by the well-armed soldiers. Most wanted to attack the Metal People before they reached the Pueblo and hopefully beat them back as they had done twelve years earlier during the revolt. But some felt it best if the Metal People were welcomed back peacefully, and some type of accommodation reached that would avoid a bloody battle. They pointed out that though the Pueblos had officially abandoned the Metal People's religious teachings, many Indians still practiced the Christian rites they had learned from their priests. There was also some talk of the mounting number of raids from other Indians, such as the Comanche, and the help the Metal People provided in fighting off the ravaging aggressors. After several hours of talk, Wise Father had, much to the annoyance of the War Chiefs, refused to approve a plan of attack. He told the gathering that he would spend the night in prayer and thought, and decide by the following morning. I asked Cactus when they expected the Metal People to arrive. Not until the following afternoon, according to Lonewolf, he answered. They had made camp for the night a few miles southwest of the Pueblo, and would probably march into Santa Fe the following day.

By the time I had finished questioning Cactus, it was late in the evening. I made my way to bed and considered what he had said. The options open to Wise Father were few. He could fight a battle that would leave many dead, or he could welcome back the Metal People, and with them, the terrible treatment of our people.

I tossed in my blankets for several hours, sometimes slipping into a confused state of half-sleep, only to find myself wide awake a few moments later. It was during one of these moments, while listening to the steady breathing of the sleeping children around me, that a disturbance in the plaza brought everyone out of their slumber. I rose quickly and crowded to the window with the other children. Shadowy figures on horseback moved among the *hornos* in the plaza. I heard my breath catch in my throat as the light from the waning moon reflected on metal worn by some of the shifting silhouettes.

It was the Metal People. They had not waited to march on the Pueblo as Lonewolf had anticipated, but instead had come in the early hours of the new day.

Wise Father was suddenly by my side with Deer Dancer. "Come quickly," he said calmly, but with a sense of urgency to his voice. "Follow Deer Dancer into the inner rooms."

Deer Dancer moved toward the door, leading the children into a short corridor that connected to the windowless rooms used to store dried corn and other vegetables. I stayed back with Wise Father until they had crossed the threshold and then we followed behind. The ceiling of the corridor was not the same height of the ceilings in the room, but had been built to the same level as the second floor roof. Long, thin open windows had been made into the wall above us to allow light to enter the corridor. A ladder made from the thin poles of young trees was pushed up against one of the windows and Lonewolf, followed by several other warriors, was climbing up and over the sill onto the roof of the first floor. The children were pushing through an open door at the end of the corridor and I started to follow them. Then I saw Wise Father making his way toward the ladder. I hesitated a moment and decided to stay with him. He sent a worried glance my way and started to speak, but then seemed to change his mind and instead climbed up the ladder and through the window. I hurried behind him, and a moment later we were standing on the edge of the roof looking down into the plaza.

Two large mounds of wood had been piled in the center of the plaza and I could see some of the soldiers frantically trying to light them. A few seconds later the first tongues of flame began to light the plaza. The wood was dry and the flames soon danced high into the night, casting a dull orange light onto the bearded faces of the Metal People. We stood watching as the men on horseback formed a line twenty paces behind the burning wood. The yells between the Metal People ceased and the plaza was silent except for the crackling of the fires and the snorting of the horses.

As we stared down from above, two soldiers dismounted and detached themselves from the main group, moving forward with their horses until they were positioned in the empty space between the fires. One led a tall gray horse, the other a smaller animal with a white marking on its forehead. I did not know who the rider on the gray horse was, but there was no mistaking the young man next to him.

11

The *Entrada*

Governor de Vargas decided to leave all but two of the wagons at the campsite. Now, under the cover of night, was the time for speed and stealth, he said, and that would be impossible if the heavy, noisy carts were brought along. The Indian drivers would follow with our supplies in the morning, after we had reached the Pueblo that had sprung up in the former capital of Santa Fe. The wagons going with us carried the two heavy cannons we had brought.

We had climbed several thousand feet in elevation during the past two days, and though it was still early September, the night air had a cold chill to it. Shortly past midnight the waning moon rose above the Sangre de Cristo Mountains in front of us. The full moon had come and gone, but it was still reflecting enough light to illuminate the piñon and juniper trees growing about us. Every once in a while the high pitched cries of coyotes were heard in the distance. They were an eerie sound, and I wished they would stop. We were already pretty high strung and it made everyone more nervous. Occasionally, in passing, we would disturb a jackrabbit, causing it to bolt out into the night in a sudden furry explosion that made the horses flinch and soldiers jump in their saddles.

We had made a gentle descent from the high volcanic perch of *La Bajada*, but the terrain started rising again as the company continued forward toward the foothills of the *Sangre de Cristo* Mountains. The Santa Fe River now ran alongside the rutted series of old trails that were the last miles of the *Camino Real*, the same one we had started upon over three hundred miles south in El Paso. Compared to the Rio Grande, the Santa Fe River looked to me more like a stream than a river. But torn trees and driftwood piled high on the banks painted a picture of gentle flowing waters that at times became a raging flood.

At the governor's instruction, we rode four abreast, forming a column that reminded me of a trail of ants. The governor led the company with del Charco, Lieutenants Campos and Montoya, and myself riding directly behind him. Some sort of military protocol determined the order. If the governor fell in battle, del Charco would take command. At least that is what the governor had told the soldiers, but I was pretty sure he also wanted del Charco close by so he could keep an eye on him.

The governor had explained his plan to the soldiers before we started marching. We were to approach the Pueblo buildings and form a battle line in the plaza in front of it. Our swords were to remain in our scabbards and our side arms holstered. He also ordered that the wicked looking lances carried by the men stay pointed into the air. Maybe my words earlier in the day had swayed him, or maybe he decided to stick with his original plan. Either way, the strategy for the reconquest had been set. The governor would try to parlay with the Indians. But the soldiers were to stand at the ready. If Governor de Vargas should release his sword from its scabbard, the soldiers were to attack.

He had also given me my orders. Everyone looked at me and I shifted uncomfortably, when the governor told the company that I, and I alone, would accompany him when he made the initial approach to the Pueblo. Both del Charco and Father Chavez had voiced concern about his decision. As second in command, del Charco felt that he should accompany the governor during this critical moment. Father Chavez, as the chief representative of the church, thought he should be the one accompanying the governor in negotiations with the Indians. But both arguments were summarily dismissed. To del Charco he gave no explanation—orders were orders, no ifs, ands or buts about it. With Father Chavez he explained his reasoning. The governor felt that a young man such as myself would help convince the Indians that his plea for a peaceful settlement was sincere. The church, on the other hand, was a strong symbol of what the Pueblos had revolted against, and would send the wrong signal. Father Chavez seemed to recognize the wisdom of his plan and agreed to stand back.

We reached Santa Fe at about four in the morning. Our final approach had been slow and quiet, but as the soldiers entered the plaza, the dark silent building that had once been the Palace of the Governors came to life with warning cries from the Indians. In front of the pueblo was the same type of mud ovens that I had seen in the abandoned pueblos along the Rio Grande. Beside the ovens were neatly stacked piles of juniper and piñon wood. Lieutenant Montoya issued a curt order and four soldiers jumped from their horses and began stacking the wood into two piles in the center of the plaza. The small logs were lit, and within a few minutes the flames shot up into the night. In their flickering light, I could see that the second story of the pueblo was set back, or terraced, on top of the first story. I got my first look at the Indians as they spilled out of the second story windows and onto the roof. Some clutched spears, others short axes. A few held large, heavy muzzle-loading firearms that I had learned were called harquebus.

The soldiers, as they had been instructed, formed a tight line in front of the building. The cannons were rolled off the wagons and positioned in plain view of the Indians, but they were not directed at the pueblo. The governor and I moved our horses to a point in front of the men. We were about fifty yards from the front doors of the pueblo, with the fires burning midway between us and the Indians. Del Charco, Lieutenants Campos and Montoya, and Father Chavez took their positions immediately behind us. Next to them, two soldiers held long, brass trumpets, and two others held small round drums supported by thin cords around their necks.

After a few minutes, the warning cries from within the pueblo died away and the noise of the mounted soldiers positioning themselves into formation stopped. Both sides stared intently at each other over the top of the fires. A sense of pent up energy filled the air. It was as if a giant mousetrap had been set, and the smallest move would bring everything crashing down upon us.

Governor de Vargas gave an almost imperceptible nod, and he and I dismounted and walked forward until we stood in the empty space between the two crackling fires. The governor then lifted his right hand and the brassy blare of the horns and the rat-a-tap-tap of the drums shattered the silence. They played on for about a minute, and then stopped as abruptly as they had started. The soldiers broke the sudden quiet as they yelled:

"Glory be to the Blessed Sacrament of the Altar!"

This set the Indians off and they now milled about in a renewed show of excitement, shaking their weapons in the air above them. They were all yelling at once and their voices became a roar vibrating with fury.

An old man stood silently in the middle of the activity. He seemed oblivious to the men around him. A young girl, about fourteen or fifteen years old, stood beside him. She was the only female, or child, among them.

Suddenly she grabbed the old man's sleeve, and he bent down and listened as she spoke in his ear. His head turned my way and they both looked at me intently. The governor caught their abrupt movement and he gave me a quick glance. But before he could say anything, the old man straightened up and made a slow sideways motion with his hand. At the gesture, the Indians fell silent.

"Who are you, and why do you threaten us?" he called out in a loud and firm voice. He spoke haltingly in Spanish, as if searching his memory for words that had not been used in many years.

"We do not come to threaten you," the governor responded. "I am Governor Don Diego de Vargas, and I have come as an emissary of his majesty, the King of Spain. I have come to seek peace with the Pueblos. I have come to seek peace that will allow us to live together, not as enemies, but as friends."

"We have lived with you in the past. We know of the peace you bring. It is a peace that enslaves our bodies and crushes our spirits. You are not welcome here," the old man replied.

"What has happened in the past, should be buried in the past," the governor said. "It is now time to look to the future. A future where the flag of Spain may fly over all that live here."

"The future you describe is the past we wish to forget," the old man replied calmly. "Yes, we have lived under your flag. And though we lived, we were also dying. Our way of life is not the same as yours. You forced on us a manner of living that would end us as a people. Go, so that we may continue to live in the way that is ours."

"As I said, that is the past," the governor said. "Your way of life is yours. Whatever wrongs were done will be righted. Accept the rule of the king, and you will be allowed to live as you have done since the beginning."

"Allowed? We do not want to exist in the servitude that you *allow* us. We are a people whose way of life is ours because it is so—not because it is allowed," the old man said.

The governor rubbed the beard on his chin in a thoughtful manner. "Perhaps my tongue does not speak the words that I am trying to say," he said at last. "In the past we have tried to change you, to make you as we are. That was wrong and many of your people and our people have died because of the ill-chosen policies forced upon the Pueblos. No longer will that be so. Your people have gods and spirits that are not the same as ours. I do not understand them or what they mean to your people. But that no longer matters. What is important is that they are the deities of your fathers and your fathers' fathers. If you should choose to accept the rule of the Empire, you will worship your gods, without interference, in the ways that are yours."

"I hear your words, but you speak as a soldier," the old man responded. He raised his hand and pointed to Father Chavez and the other friars mounted on their horses in a group behind the governor. "Do you also speak for your holy men?"

Governor de Vargas turned to Father Chavez and beckoned him to join us. Del Charco stiffened, and seemed to be mumbling under his breath. Father Chavez dismounted and walked forward until he stood next to us.

"In the past, our priests confused you by issuing policies that differed from those spoken by the government established in Santa Fe by the king," Father Chavez said. "These differences came about when both the men of the church and of the government fought to exercise control over your people. The results of these actions helped to create the environment that led to the Pueblo's revolt. We have learned from our errors, and assure you that the church now supports the promises put forth by Governor de Vargas. Our doors are thrown open to you, and we hope that you will join with us in worship of our God—just as many of you have done in the past. But we will no longer stand in the way if you choose to practice your religion in the tradition of your people."

The old man listened carefully and then began describing the wrongs that had befallen his people since the arrival of the Spaniards. The list was long, and he spoke at length, without any interruption. He described the hard labor they were forced to endure, the treatment of the women and children, and of the hunger and starvation inflicted upon his people when the soldiers took from them the crops they grew in the fields. He talked of the systematic destruction of their religion—the burning of the *kivas*, the banning of their ceremonies and the imprisonment of the Pueblos' religious leaders. His voice dropped when he described the humiliation, torture and executions that were wrought in the name of God, and in the tradition of Spanish justice.

While he spoke, I studied the girl standing motionless at his side, trying to see her face more clearly. But in the shadows cast by the roaring fires, her features remained hidden.

After the old man finished talking, Governor de Vargas spoke again. He addressed each of the points brought up by the old Indian and reassured him that the wrongs would not be repeated. While he was talking the eastern sky took on a soft pinkish tinge and by the time the governor was through speaking, the first rays of the morning sun were striking the tops of the trees along the river valley.

I could see the girl more clearly now. Her skin was a dark brown like the other Indians and her jet-black hair hung down below her shoulders. I noted her upturned nose and strong chin when she turned in profile. The old man leaned over to whisper in her ear and the tension in her stand relaxed for a moment, and she laughed at whatever he had said. As she laughed, her hand came up and covered her mouth.

I gave an involuntary start. It was a gesture I had seen hundreds of times before. Suddenly our eyes met and her hand came down. She smiled at me and gave a tiny wave. I felt a strange giddiness in my stomach and gave her a big grin.

189

Wise Father placed his arm around my shoulders as he described the stealing of our children, mostly young girls of my age, by the Metal People. He spoke of the useless tokens the parents were given as payment for the stolen children. How could the Spaniards ever think, he asked of the man called de Vargas, that material goods would diminish the grief and rage felt by the Pueblo over a forever-lost child?

The two men had been talking back-and-forth for hours. I felt Wise Father growing tired, but he refused to sit, and instead remained standing. Their words were in the strange language of the Spaniards—a tongue I had never heard Wise Father use before.

In the two days before the arrival of the Metal People, I had spent my waking hours with the people of the other pueblos and had only begun to learn the basic words of their speech. But by the time the sun had risen, I understood everything that was being said between Wise Father and de Vargas. I did not understand how this could be. It was one more peculiar thing to try and fit in with the visions, the dreams, and, now, the appearance of my dream brother. Only he was no longer my dream brother, he was my real brother: A brother from a different place, but my brother all the same.

Several hours passed before he knew me. At first he had given me a curious look, and then, as the hours passed, he stared with growing intensity. I waved at him when I knew he had finally recognized me. When he smiled back, a flood of memories of the other place washed over me. I did not know what they meant, but I wasn't concerned about it anymore.

That my worry had disappeared was perhaps odd, but I knew that these unusual events were beyond my control, and what would come, would come. In some ways it was like the beginning of the growing season. Many of my Pueblo Brothers would look to the sky at the planting of the seeds and worry about the summer rains. I always felt that was unnecessary. The rains would come or not, and all the wasted thoughts could not change what the Water People sent to us.

Wise Father and de Vargas talked until mid-morning. By that time many of the soldiers and their horses had become tired and restless. The line they formed in front of the pueblo was no longer as straight and rigid as it had been. Finally, Wise Father and de Vargas were silent. They had both said what they thought needed to be said. After a long moment, Wise Father announced that the two groups needed time to consider what had passed. De Vargas agreed, and he and Carlos turned and walked from the smoldering embers of the fires to the soldiers waiting behind them. We climbed down the ladders into the corridor and made our way to one of the big rooms in the pueblo.

Once there, Wise Father stepped to the front of the room and faced the gathering of warriors. I leaned back against the thick adobe wall and felt the coolness of its surface through my dress. The leaders of the other villages had remained silent while Wise Father spoke from the roof to the soldier, de Vargas. But in the room, away from the Metal People, they began a discussion among themselves that was much like the one Cactus had described to me earlier.

Many felt that any more talk would be of no use. Now, while the Spaniards rested, was an opportunity to attack the soldiers and send them running back to the land from which they came. The Metal People's words, they said, were like the mist of the river—seen in the early morning, but disappearing under the light of day. The white men could not be trusted, and to believe their promises was to invite the terrible ways of the past back into the Pueblos.

The Metal People could have struck with their superior weapons while we slept, said others. But they did not. That is because they need a peaceful coexistence. They recognize that the true enemies—the Apache and other marauding tribes—cannot be defeated if there is not peace from within. We speak of preserving our way of life, they continued, but is not our way of life in danger because our numbers diminish and we are growing to weak to defend our village? The strength of the Metal People need not be loosed upon us when instead it can defend our people as it did in the past.

And so again the talk went back-and-forth. Wise Father and Lonewolf did not speak, but listened patiently to those who chose to have their voice heard. When all who wished to speak had done so, Wise Father turned to where Lonewolf stood against the opposite wall and nodded at him. Lonewolf stepped forward and his eyes swept over the men before him. He paused when he saw me. I think he was surprised. No other women were present, and certainly not any of the children.

"There is much to be considered from what we have heard," he finally said with an edge of uncertainty in his voice. The uncertainty surprised me. It was not Lonewolf's way to speak in such a manner. He was always confident when advising Wise Father. The Pueblo could always take encouragement from the strength of his words.

"Those that know me," he continued, "know that I have no fear of our enemies—whether it be Indians or the

 192

Metal People. I believe that if we go into battle with the Metal People, the greater force of our people will triumph. But I also believe if we defeat them now, it will not be the end of them. Just as they have returned to us today, they will do so in the future. And each time they return it will be in greater numbers. With their horses, weapons and metal coats, there will come a time when we will no longer be victorious. On that day, our way of life—our religion, our language and the people we are—will cease to be. This leader of the Metal People makes promises that will let us continue to live in the manner that we must. I do not know if these promises are real or if they will disappear once this time is past. They give no guarantee, but what guarantee could they give that is greater than their word."

Lonewolf paused and his eyes fixed upon Wise Father. "You must be the judge of the truth in their words. If you find in your heart that they are hollow, then know that I am ready, and we are prepared, to meet them in battle now. All of us will stand with our weapons close, and be ready to fight at any time.

"But if you find truth in their words, I am ready to lay down my weapons, and welcome them as part of the way of our world."

Many voices tried to be heard when Lonewolf finished speaking. The War Chief of one of the *Keres* Pueblos to the south climbed upon a bench and all became silent listening to his words.

"We have the strength of numbers," he exclaimed forcefully, "and we must attack now. These white devils respect and fear only one thing, and that is the terror that we can rain down upon them. If they feel the fury of our weap-

193

ons, if they are forced to flee like the rabbit before the coyote, then they will never dare come into our lands again. That is the only course of action we can take. It is the only thing they understand. To do otherwise is to condemn ourselves to a slow death under the weight of their laws and their church.

"We have the might to finish this now! Let us do so!"

I saw many warriors murmuring among themselves and nodding in agreement with the War Chief's words. Wise Father lifted his hands and everyone became silent.

"When I was much younger, no older than Sage," he said, nodding toward me, "the oldest men in the Pueblo told stories about the coming of the Metal People. For two growing seasons they were here with our fathers. As is our way, they were greeted and welcomed into our villages. At first they were friendly and moved comfortably among us. But their ways soon became harsh, and there was much celebration among our people when they finally left. Then, after over forty summers had passed..." He paused and his eyes had a distant look.

"They returned," he murmured, as if to himself. Suddenly his eyes focused on the men gathered before him and he spoke in a loud strong voice. "Lonewolf is right. Just as they returned before, they will return again. Now they come to us offering friendship and freedom. I fear that if we send them fleeing, as we did before, they will some day be among us again. It may not be in my lifetime, or in the lifetime of those gathered here today. But there will come a time when our children, or our children's children, will encounter them again. The responsibility is with us to bury the animosity if we are able.

"Keep your weapons at hand, for I do not know where the return of the Metal People will lead us. But I am ready to continue talking with the leader called de Vargas, and work to bring peace between our peoples."

The War Chief opened his mouth to speak, but before he could say anything, he was interrupted by a disturbance at one of the doors leading into the room. It was Cactus and all eyes turned to him.

"They have shut off the water to the pueblo!" he cried. "They have blocked the ditch carrying the water that feeds us!"

An angry buzz filled the room and the men lifted their spears and bows and began shaking them. Wise Father stared at Cactus with an incredulous expression on his face.

"It is as I said," cried the *Keresan* War Chief. "The Metal People cannot be trusted! Let us storm them now and send them running back to their great king in the far off land!"

Wise Father looked out over the room. "Wait!" he said in a voice filled with a power that I had never heard before. All voices were quieted as he asserted his leadership. "We must take our positions in preparation for battle, but first I will speak with de Vargas and search for the meaning of this abominable action.

"Return to your places on the roof, while I go into the plaza." Wise Father paused for a short moment, looking at the *Keresan* War Chief. "The seeds of war have taken root, but we shall not lift our arms until there is no other path open to us."

The *Keresan* opened his mouth as though to speak, but then seemed to think better of it. Instead he turned and quickly left the room, with the other men following behind him. We could hear them moving down the corridor and up the ladders leading to the roof. In a short time Wise Father and I stood alone. Suddenly, the learned man—the gummy bear man—was talking to Carlos and me in a vision or memory. I was no longer sure which. He was telling us that this dispute ended peacefully. I felt confused. How could he have told us how it ended, when it hadn't yet begun? A tremble ran through my body and I felt my legs go weak as I answered my silent question. *The world I shared with Carlos was not only in another place, but also in another time.*

Wise Father had started across the room, but he sensed my shiver. He stopped and turned, looking at me with his patient eyes and an expression of concern furrowing his brow. Before he could speak, I told him of my vision. He did not show any surprise at my words of a different time, but was instead much more interested in the meaning of the gummy bear man's words. He had me repeat them twice. When I had finished, he stared at me thoughtfully. After a moment, we turned and walked together through a door, opposite the one leading into the corridor, and into the entry leading to the plaza. At the front door he hesitated for a moment and I thought he was going to ask another question of me. But instead he opened the door and we stepped into the afternoon brightness of the plaza. I squinted and brought my hand to my brow so as to shield my eyes until they had adjusted to the brightness of the sun.

Ten paces in front of us stood de Vargas and Carlos. De Vargas held his metal helmet in his hands. A soldier, smaller than those mounted in the line across the plaza, stood next to them.

I looked at the soldier in surprise. I had not known before that their women also dressed in armor.

12

Waiting

"You were looking bored," Governor de Vargas said with a grin that showed strong white teeth against his sunburned skin. The sun had risen and the governor and the old man had finally stopped talking. It had been at least six or seven hours since the horns and drums had announced the company's arrival and I was feeling tired as we trudged to the side of the plaza opposite the Palace of the Governors turned Indian village.

"Well," I said, talking as we walked, "it was exciting at first, when we blew the trumpets and all the Indians came rushing onto the roof. But then you and the old Indian man both kept repeating yourselves. You just said the same things over and over to each other."

The governor laughed. "Welcome to your

first taste of diplomacy, Carlos. Actually, I should say your second taste."

"What was the first?" I asked, not understanding what he meant.

"Sometimes diplomacy is a message that may be sent symbolically. In this case, I was attempting to send two messages. The first bit of diplomacy was when I approached the pueblo with you. Did you see how the old man looked at you?" I thought the old man stared at me because of something Sage said, but I kept that to myself and listened as the governor continued speaking. "Your youth and stature helped create a somewhat benign tableau. Can you imagine if I had brought Lieutenant Campos with me? One look at that frightening behemoth, and our whole appearance would have been one of cruel, brutal strength. With just the two of us, the initial fear they probably had of an immediate attack was set aside. But the line of soldiers backing us up also told them that the door is open to forceful action if an accommodation cannot be reached. With that dual message they were willing to listen to what I had to say. Then they could talk and I could talk and they could talk again and I could talk again. It is frustratingly slow, but if it avoids bloodshed, it is worth the time taken."

Del Charco didn't think it was worth the time taken and he lit into the governor as soon as we had moved away from the pueblo.

"This is going nowhere," he said with cold anger in his voice. "What is the use of talking to these savages? They will only let us have the palace if we show them the edge of our swords and the back of our hands. All the Indians are now inside. We should waste no time in attacking. Let us catch them unprepared and victory will be ours!"

The governor took a deep breath and stared at del Charco with an expression of utter contempt.

"I know what you want, Captain," he said through clenched teeth. "You want to pound these people into submission and control them as you do your poor horse.

"But can you not see? Are you blind to the circumstances leading up to this campaign? These are people who have lived here for hundreds, nay, for thousands of years. Maybe we can claim victory today, but that will not extinguish the flames of anger first ignited almost a hundred years ago. Yes, we can make them ours for a while, but the resentment will continue to live and grow, and they will revolt again. Is that what you desire? Centuries of fighting and death?

"I wish to resolve this once and for all" de Vargas continued, "and the only resolution that will avoid acrimony and hate is to bring these people and the Spanish Crown together in a manner that allows them to live as they need to— in a manner that allows them to be the people they are. Then they will be comfortable within our rule. To do otherwise will mean a continuation of the animosity that caused our people to flee and die during the revolt twelve years ago. Do you not see this? What is it in you that demands violence and blood to be satisfied?"

Del Charco was silent for a moment like a child who had been chastised. But he wasn't a child, and his eyes blazed in a frightening manner.

"Governor de Vargas," he finally said, "you have put our objective and the men of this company at risk. Are we to just sit here and wait? For a day? A week? Will we still be sitting here when the snows of winter have covered our boots? You must do something more. You must show these savages that we are ready to act in earnest. To do otherwise is to continue the erroneous policies you have already initiated. Policies, I must add, that will be carefully noted in my report to the vice royalty. The success of our campaign, or lack of, is upon your head."

"As it should be, Captain," responded the governor in a level voice. "You are of course free to report as you wish, but you will follow my orders. We will only engage the Indians when all other courses of action have failed."

Del Charco gave a sigh of exasperation and turned to Lieutenant Montoya, who stood silently during the exchange between the two men. "Are you a post to which the horses may be tied?" Del Charco asked bitterly, causing Lieutenant Montoya to stiffen. "Do you not have a tongue? You are a military man. What is your advice on this matter? Speak now."

"The lieutenant is my aide, Captain," interrupted the governor, "I will take his counsel when I deem it appropriate. That is all, Captain. Rest now, but stay close."

"So that you may ensure I follow your orders? Do not worry, Governor. I am a soldier, accustomed to following orders. I will not attack the heathens until I hear your command. I can only hope that it will be soon in coming."

Del Charco walked away and we all watched as he began an animated conversation with Lieutenant Campos. Governor de Vargas stared after him and then turned to Lieutenant Montoya.

"Now it is your time to speak. Am I wrong? What words of advice do you offer?"

Lieutenant Montoya hesitated a moment before speaking. "Though I wish it were otherwise, Governor, I am forced to agree with del Charco on one matter. We cannot stand here

200

indefinitely. The soldiers have now gone without sleep for one night. They are strong, but they will need to rest sooner or later. To retire in front of the Indians will send a signal that our resolve has weakened. I am not advocating an attack on the palace, but something must be done to bring this to a close."

The governor rubbed his brow as he contemplated what the lieutenant had said.

"Your reasoning leaves little room for argument, Lieutenant. But, we must make sure that any action we take does not start us down a path from which there is no turning back. One misstep, and a calamity will rain down upon us."

The governor and Lieutenant Montoya moved off to the shade of a cottonwood tree to discuss the options open to them. A line of soldiers continued to hold in formation in front of the pueblo, but several others had been allowed to fall back and rest a few hundred yards to the south in the shade of the trees along the riverbank. I saw Sofía sitting by herself and led Estrella over to her. She smiled as I approached, and the weight of the pressure surrounding me seemed a bit lighter.

"So, did you tell them what they must do?" she asked.

"No, I didn't say anything. We were just trying to decide what to do next...," I stopped speaking when I saw the sparkle of amusement in her eyes and realized she was teasing me. "What are you laughing about? This is pretty important, you know."

"I know it is and I'm sorry, Carlos," she said, trying to put a serious expression to her face, "but I can't get over you sitting with the governor discussing the fate of the campaign."

Then suddenly her voice was serious. "You really have come a long way from the little boy I used to know—both in the way you speak and the way you act. You are becoming a man. The life we had, where I looked after you, where I played with you like an older sister, is almost gone. Soon all I will have is the memories of our youth."

I stared at her trying to keep a blank look from coming to my face. I had absolutely no memory of being a little boy with her. This is probably what a person with amnesia feels like, I thought—a whole other life that can't be remembered. I suppose it is harder on those that have lived for years with you, than those who have no recollection of what has passed. I wondered if Sage was experiencing the same thing inside the pueblo with the Indians.

"I know I have changed a lot in the last month," I said slowly. "And so have you, and so has everybody else around us. Who wouldn't be changed by the journey we've traveled, and the things we've seen? Our relationship isn't the same as it was. It is different, but it will be as strong as ever. Maybe even stronger than before."

Sofía gave me a sad little smile but didn't say anything. I had an urge to take her hand in mine, but didn't. There were soldiers lounging close by, and it would have looked pretty weird if anyone saw me doing that. Instead I placed my hand gently on her shoulder. Then she reached up and placed her hand upon mine. She grasped it tightly for a brief second, before withdrawing it. Her eyes met mine and I saw a sparkle that made my stomach flutter.

"So anyway," I continued, changing the subject in a voice that sounded a little ragged, "here is what is going on." I gave her the details of the argument between del Charco and the governor, and why the governor had chosen to take me with him when he addressed the Indians. She didn't have much to say after I finished.

Then I took a deep breath and told her I had found Sage. This news caused her to sit up straight and give me a wide-eyed look. She had of course seen the Indian girl standing with the old man, and I told her how I had come to recognize Sage; even in her Indian dress and with long black hair flowing past her shoulders.

"Are you really sure it was her, Carlos?" she asked doubtfully, her brow furrowing in concentration. "Maybe you are so eager to find your sister, that you just think you see her in that young girl."

"No, Sofía," I said, shaking my head. "You know, there are a lot of things I am unsure of in this strange place, but of this, I am certain. That Indian girl is my sister. She doesn't look quite the same, but it is Sage."

Sofía lay back slowly until she was staring up at the tree branches directly above us. I did the same and crossed my arms beneath my head. There was a moment of silence before she spoke.

"If what you believe is really true," she finally said in a thick voice, "then you don't belong here. You belong in another place far from here." She paused. "How will you get back there?"

"I wish I knew, Sofía. Maybe when all this mess is over."

She didn't respond and I remained silent. After a few minutes I looked over at her. Her eyes were closed and she was breathing evenly. Even in her armor, with dust and soot from the fires on her cheeks, she looked prettier to me than she had back in El Paso, which didn't make much sense. I looked up at the leaves rustling in the breeze above us. So much had happened, and the rainy Thanksgiving evening that had started this wild journey seemed so long ago. The dangerous march across the *Jornada del Muerto*, the incredible thirst I had felt, and even the murdered Indian family, were now memories. Maybe Sage and I would be here forever, but I didn't really think so. That was a sad thought, though. I didn't want Sofía to ever become just a memory.

I must have fallen asleep. All of a sudden I awoke abruptly to someone calling my name. I sat up and saw Sofía shaking her head and rubbing her eyes next to me. She had the confused look one gets when awakened from a deep sleep. I probably had the same expression on my face. The governor stood a few feet away staring at us. I guessed, from the shadow of the tree, that we had slept for a couple of hours. It looked to be about three o'clock in the afternoon.

"I need the two of you to come with me," he said when he noticed that we were fully awake. "Nothing seems to be happening in there and we cannot wait much longer. Therefore, I am going to try and give them a nudge by blocking the ditch carrying water from the river to the pueblo."

His words swept the last cobwebs of sleep from my mind. Suddenly I was wide awake. "That doesn't sound like a nudge, Governor," I blurted out. "That sounds more like a punch in the stomach. How can you be sure that won't bring the Indians swarming out of the pueblo like angry wasps?"

"I don't know that they won't," he said grimly. "I'm pretty sure there will be some in the pueblo who will advocate the response you describe. That is why I need the two of you. I need to show that our intent is still peaceful, that our damming of their water is not meant as an act designed to cause war."

"What do you mean?" Sofía asked. I noted that she spoke in her normal voice, no longer trying to disguise it with the deep baritone she had used up until now. Maybe she was still half asleep and forgot to do it. The governor didn't show any sign that he noticed the change.

"I don't have time to explain right now. The men are stopping the water flow as we speak. We need to get to the pueblo. Follow me quickly," he ordered in a voice that left no room for more questions. We hurried across the plaza to the empty space between the fires we had lit the night before. The governor removed his sword and leaned it against one of the *hornos*. I could see that Lieutenant Montoya had been busy. All the men were once again lined up in formation in front of the pueblo.

Suddenly the Indians began to gather on the pueblo roof, and if they had been angry before, it was nothing compared to the way they were now. They began taunting us with words I didn't understand, but whose meaning was clear. The soldiers stared back at them and, for the most part, showed no emotion on their faces, but their hands were white at the knuckles from the tight grip they had on their spears. The noise the Indians created caused the horses to shift nervously and their ears lay flat against their heads.

The front door of the pueblo opened and Sage walked out with the old man. They stopped a few paces from us, and the Indians became silent. I looked at Sage, and she looked at me. I was at a loss as to what to do. It had probably been six weeks since I had last seen her at Doctor Lopez's and I suppose I should have rushed over and given her a quick hug at least. But in the heavy silence that surrounded us in the dusty plaza with soldiers and Indians facing off for what could be a bloody battle, it would have been out of place.

"Hi, Sage," I said instead.

"Hello, Dream Brother Carlos," she replied. We both

spoke in English, which caused both the old man and the governor to start in surprise. But before we could say anything more, the air filled with the low, heavy pom-pom-pom of beating drums. The sound seemed to be coming from a round structure that I'd been told was the Pueblo's *Kiva*. As if on cue, the old man and the governor turned their heads from Sage and me, and stared at each other.

"You have stopped the flow of water into our village," the old man said, his eyes narrowing as he spoke. "That was a very foolish if you truly wish to have peace with us." His voice was loud enough to rise above the low thump of the drums, but disappeared for a moment as the Indians on roof started yelling again. Their cries continued to rise until the drums could just barely be heard. The old man looked up over his shoulder at the men on the roof above him, and stepped closer to us.

"I have stopped the attack of our warriors for the moment," he yelled, trying to be heard over the noise, "but I fear that their anger will soon spill over like the river during a summer storm. And if that should happen, I will no longer be able to contain their fury. The war chiefs shall do what they feel must be done."

I glanced up at the Indians and then back at Sage. It looked to me like the warriors were preparing to climb over the edge of the roof and begin their attack. It wasn't going at all the way Doctor Lopez had described back in the Great Room.

But it also wasn't my war. I started looking around and making my plans for escape. It would only take me a second to grab Sage, then about three seconds to reach Estrella. Maybe, if I moved fast enough, we could ride out of this place before the battle. But how about Sofía? Could I grab her also, and spirit the both of them away? And where would we go? El Paso was far away, and all I had was the pack on Estrella's back. The few pieces of beef jerky in it wouldn't keep us going for very long. Certainly not long enough to get us across the *Jornada del Muerto.* And what if Sage didn't want to go. I had grown to like and admire the governor during the past weeks and I wondered for a brief moment if Sage had become close to her people in the same way. The questions were running through my head faster than I could even start to answer them.

Then events took a strange twist.

"I am Governor Don Diego de Vargas," the governor cried in a voice that rose above the noise. "I have assured you that I come in peace, and my words are true." He turned to Sofía and fumbled with the leather strap holding her helmet in place. Sofía's hands came up and grasped his wrists, trying to stop him. He looked into her eyes and gave a small nod of his head. Her hands slowly dropped to her side. Quickly he loosened the helmet and turned until he was facing the old man and the Indians on the roof.

"If I did not wish peace between us," he yelled out, "if I was not sincere in promising you the freedoms that will avoid war, would I have come to you with a boy," he said pointing at me and then turning back to the old man, "and with a woman at my side." Had he been an actor, his timing would have probably earned him an Academy Award. With one fluid motion, he removed the helmet from Sofía's head, and her long brown hair dropped to her shoulders.

The drums continued to beat from within the *Kiva*, but the yells abruptly stopped.

All eyes were on Sofía.

13

Into Sage's Pueblo

I stared at Wise Father, wondering why he and our people were so surprised. The first time I saw her I had known immediately that she was a woman, but it seemed that I was alone in recognizing this. Even the soldiers, lined up at attention in front of our pueblo, were taken aback. I looked at Carlos. but it was apparent that he had known her true identity all along.

The force of our people's anger was replaced by a sense of curious amazement brought on by the contradictions in de Vargas' actions. First he had deprived us of water, but then had come forth, without his sword and with a woman at his side. In the village, when the time for fighting was upon us, the women and children were always left behind, and a warrior's weapons were always held close.

208

"It is a trick!" yelled the war chief of the *Keresans*. "Let us attack now, or surely all we are shall be lost!"

Wise Father looked over his shoulder at the war chief and stared at him for a moment. The rumbling of the other warriors rose again at his cry, but astonishment muted the strength of their yells. Then Wise Father lifted his hand and signaled with an outstretched palm that they should wait. The warriors became silent as they watched to see how Wise Father would react to this unforeseen behavior. Though the immediate threat of battle seemed to have been averted, the drums still continued their slow methodical beat.

Wise Father turned back toward de Vargas, and the two men studied each other.

"Why?" Wise Father asked. "Why, if you wish to have peace, do you bring us to the point where violent confrontation is almost unavoidable?"

"There are those you lead who demand war," de Vargas said, with a quick glance at the *Keresan* war chief. "As with you, I have those who believe the force of battle is the only answer to the situation we now find ourselves in. I risk war to satisfy their demands, but it is a risk I must take. I can only hope that the wisdom of your years and my desire for peace will rise above these pressures that are not of our making."

Wise Father did not answer, but after a moment of thought, nodded in understanding. Then, as if ignoring the events of the last few minutes, he began speaking again of the past injustices brought upon our villages by the Metal People. I saw the corners of de Vargas' mouth turn up in the barest suggestion of a smile. Wise Father was using the skills learned during his many years. He was draining the anger and hostility with more talk, and de Vargas realized this. Taking his direction from Wise Father, he responded with promises of a new way of life. Then the two men exchanged words in the same manner as they had done during the early morning hours.

I stared intently at Carlos and he at me as they spoke. Many new thoughts—no, not thoughts, but memories—of my time with him in the other world flowed through my mind. They were like water in a rising river. First starting slowly, and then coursing through me in a mighty torrent. I now knew the other world, and I now knew it to be real. It was no longer a dream.

Several more hours passed. It looked like there would be no end to the exchange, until finally de Vargas asked of Wise Father what could be done in order to reach the peace they both desired. Wise Father thought long and hard before answering.

"You wish us to accept the promises of your people," he said finally, "but before the Metal People can gain our trust, you, as their leader, must demonstrate to our many villages that you truly wish to walk among us in peace."

"I am ready to do whatever it takes," de Vargas said. "Tell me what will bring us together as one."

Wise Father hesitated before answering. "Come into our home and greet the people of the village. Come without your soldiers. Come alone with just the two of them," he said, indicating with a nod Carlos and the woman dressed as a soldier.

I sensed that Wise Father's suggestion caused de Vargas some alarm, but his face displayed no sign of his thoughts. He turned to Carlos and the woman and leaned his head slightly to one side while his eyes seemed to query them. They looked at de Vargas, then to each other. As one, they looked back and nodded. They were willing to join him within the walls of our pueblo. De Vargas turned back to Wise Father.

"Will you guarantee our safety?" he asked.

"That," Wise Father said, "is something I cannot promise. But I will accompany you every step of the way. I will do all that is within my power to ensure that no harm befalls you."

There could be no greater promise. With Wise Father at their side, I thought, no one would dare raise their hand against them.

"Very well," de Vargas said in a steady voice. "We will do what you think must be done."

Wise Father and I turned and walked to the door. I gave a quick glance over my shoulder, catching Carlos' eye. He raised his eyebrows in a questioning manner and smiled nervously.

Then we were inside my home.

14

What Sofia Saw

"Sofía," Carlos whispered to me, "I don't like this at all."

"You mean having the governor remove my helmet and exposing me as a woman to everyone," I said softly out of the corner of my mouth, "or going into the pueblo?"

"Exposing you kept a fight from starting. I'm talking about going into the pueblo. It's like going from the frying pan into the fire."

I was confused by his words for a moment. Then I understood his meaning. It was as if we were in a hot skillet—images of us dancing about to keep the soles of our boots from burning popped into my head—and we were leaving it to jump into the flames of the fire below.

This was not the first time Carlos had used strange words with references that I had never heard before. His unusual behavior and method of expressing himself had begun the morning I found him yelling and struggling in his sheets back in El Paso. He was the same person I had known since I first began taking care of him as a child, and then he wasn't. I became very alarmed when he told me he did not remember the life we had shared together and that he believed he was from a place three hundred years in the future. I was certain that the heat of our desert crossing had addled his brain, but having found the sister he was in search of, and seeing that she recognized him as her brother, made me question my own sanity. Perhaps the ridiculous helmet I wore as part of my soldier disguise had damaged my brain. Or maybe this horrid adventure was really a nightmare that I would soon wake from. But my mind seemed to be fine in all other respects, and I had never known a dream to be so real. So what else could it be, I asked myself. I could think of no answer, and whatever it was would have to wait. The old Indian man had started moving toward the door, with the governor and Carlos following. I whispered a quick prayer to the Virgin Mother, crossed myself, and hurried after them

A small shiver ran up my back as I peered into the murky shadows beyond the doorway. Like Carlos, I didn't want to enter the pueblo either, but there had really been no choice when the old Indian invited us in. To decline his offer would probably have ended any hope in the peace talks, and provided those wanting a fight with the final argument to engage in battle. But I also knew, by accepting the invitation and entering the pueblo without the soldiers, we would be doomed if Governor de Vargas' plan did not unfold in the manner he hoped.

The front door into the pueblo wasn't really a door at all. I could see the outline in the mud wall of the original great double door that had opened to the plaza before the palace had been transformed into a Pueblo building. After the Pueblo Revolt, the Indians had blocked the front entrance with adobe bricks, leaving only a small rectangular opening that looked like a low, narrow window frame. The old Indian man went through with Carlos' Indian sister, Sage.

The governor had to bow his head to keep it from striking the top of the frame as he stepped over the raised threshold. Carlos followed the governor and, once inside, turned and gave me his hand for support as I entered behind them.

The top of my metal helmet, placed back on my head by the governor, brushed against the top of the door frame. As part of my disguise, I had had to keep my hair pushed up underneath the helmet. It had been hot and uncomfortable. Now I could let it hang free about my shoulders instead of tucked away from sight. I wondered if Joan of Arc had felt the same. Then I thought of the end she had met. Would I find a similar fate within the walls of this building?

It was cool and dim inside the entry hall, which was probably about thirty feet long and half as wide. Leading off it were several raised doors like the one we had just come through. As we followed the old man, I glanced into the rooms. Originally, they had been large and spacious, but the Indians had changed them greatly. Most were no bigger than my bed in El Paso. A few were a bit bigger and had a small fireplace built into the wall. Soft animal skins lay in thick piles on the floor.

The old man led us from the entry hall into a large room with wooden benches lining the wall. Through the doorway at the end of the room, I could see part of a corridor with ladders propped against the wall. Several Indians whom I recognized from the rooftop were climbing down and filing one at a time into the room. Most stared at us with grim, unfriendly expressions on their faces, but a few of the younger men looked at us with curiosity. These had been children when the Pueblos had revolted.

Governor de Vargas stood patiently next to the old man until the last of the Indians had entered. Then, moving from man to man, he began introducing himself with polite words and a small bow. I don't think most of them understood what he was saying, but they seemed to relax a bit.

Sage, Carlos and I moved to a seat on one of the far benches. Sage sat between Carlos and me. They put their heads close together and exchanged a few words in English, a language I recognized but did not understand. I had been almost as surprised as the old man and the governor when they had first spoken to each other in the plaza. Prior to that moment, I still doubted whether Carlos' story of another place was really true. I had thought the place he described might be a creation of his imagination. But when they spoke in English, the last of my doubts had evaporated.

"Sofía," Carlos said, looking at me and reverting to Spanish, "this is my sister, Sage. Sage, this is Sofía."

"I am pleased to meet you, Sofía," she said in perfect Spanish. "I did not see you in the visions I had of Dream Brother."

"Um...it is my pleasure...Sage," I responded. Carlos looked at her for a brief moment with a puzzled expression before speaking.

"You've called me that twice. I'm not a dream brother," he said gently, "unless maybe you think all this is a dream. I've often thought the same thing over the past few weeks. But it is not a dream."

"Carlos," she said, speaking slowly, "the dream I speak of is of the other place, the place where you...where we, are brother and sister."

Carlos looked at her with a dumbfounded expression on his face. After a moment he spoke.

"No, Sage. That is the real place, our real world. This isn't...," he said haltingly, searching for the right words, "this isn't where we are from. How can you even think so? You've only been here for a short time. Weren't they all strangers when you first saw them?"

I felt a pain in my chest when Carlos uttered those words. It was not his fault, but nevertheless, he caused me great sorrow. All the memories I carried of us—from the time we fled the revolt to the many hours spent in comfortable conversation as we grew—were unknown to him.

"I do not know what you mean, Carlos," Sage said. "I have known the people of my village all of my life." She pointed over to the old Indian still standing next to de Vargas. "That is Wise Father, the father of my mother. He has raised me since I was very young." Then she singled out some of the other Indians and told us their names and little anecdotes about her life with them.

I was more confused than ever. If Carlos didn't remember our time together, then how was it that Sage remembered her Pueblo life? I was envious of the man called Wise Father—at least the young girl he had raised knew him.

"Don't you remember our mother?" Carlos asked.

"Yes, and with every passing hour I remember more of my life in the other world. I have memories of the place where we grew up, and of a father that left us many years ago. I also see, in my mind, the gummy bear man telling us of this place."

"Doctor Lopez, you mean," Carlos said with a smile. "You thought he looked like a gummy bear in his green raincoat."

Sage thought for a moment. "I do not know what a raincoat is, but yes, that is his name, Doctor Lopez."

Governor de Vargas and the old man called Wise Father had finished meeting with the other Indians and were moving toward a closed door between the benches. As they approached the door, they turned and stared at the three of us with an expectant look.

"I do not wish to interrupt," I said, "but I think they are waiting for us to join them."

I could see that both had more that they wanted to say. They were both exploring, trying to fit what had passed into what was to come. It was as if the danger we now shared was less important than their need to know.

I stood and walked to the governor, and they both followed reluctantly. Wise Father opened the door and we all trailed behind him as he led us into a small courtyard surrounded by the Pueblo buildings.

Standing about were many more Indians. Up until this time, all we had seen were warriors, but in the courtyard were women and children. I did not see anger in their eyes, but a mixture of worry and curiosity. If del Charco has his way, I thought, many of them will be casualties of the battle he desires. They did not know del Charco, but they realized that perilous events were unfolding around them. It was no wonder they were worried.

Governor de Vargas approached them as he had the men in the meeting room and spoke to them in a gentle voice. He continued to introduce himself, and would occasionally stop and speak quietly to the children. Sitting against the courtyard wall with a puppy in his arms was the largest Indian I had ever seen. The governor paused before him for a moment and then spoke. But the Indian paid him little attention. He was more intent on playing with the puppy. I could see from his features that he was not capable of understanding the governor's words. Governor de Vargas also realized this, and, after eliciting no response, continued circulating among the other Indians.

It was late in the afternoon before he had finished speaking to each of them. Carlos and Sage continued to talk to each other, trying to understand what the other felt. I also heard Carlos assuring her that the governor was sincere in the promises he was making. Finally, when the sun had almost disappeared in the west and the courtyard had filled with shadows, the governor and Wise Father, followed by the three of us, moved back into the pueblo. The governor's visit seemed to have been successful. Inside the meeting room, the governor and several Indians spoke at length of the life they would share in peace. The tension and anger that had greeted us was gone. It looked like the threat of bloodshed had disappeared with the setting sun.

By the time we emerged from the pueblo, the only light in the plaza was from the fires that had been rebuilt. In the red hue cast by the burning logs, I could see the soldiers standing in formation visibly relax at the sight of the smiling governor. We stood in front of the pueblo for a while longer as Wise Father and Governor de Vargas made plans to form a company of soldiers and Indians that would travel together to the other pueblos and tell them of the peace that had been reached. Carlos and Sage talked of meeting again the following morning to continue sorting out the confusing events that had passed. While the final words of parting were exchanged, many of the other Indian men gathered close, while others reappeared on the roof. I grew apprehensive at their appearance, but the hostility displayed during the day had evaporated and the pounding of the drums had ceased.

We walked across the plaza, past the fires and up to the soldiers. Governor de Vargas ordered the soldiers to dismount and stand at ease. The men began to realize what had happened and an almost jovial atmosphere surrounded the company as they stood around the governor listening intently as he described what had passed in the pueblo. The relieved smiles of the men were contagious, and I found myself smiling.

Then my eyes fell upon the hate-laced grimace of del Charco. He and Lieutenant Campos stood a few yards from the rest of the company, apart from us, but close enough to hear the governor's words. I shuddered as his face took on a deranged look unlike any I had ever seen before. I nudged Carlos' shoulder and he looked over at the Captain. The smile on his face disappeared when he saw his expression.

Suddenly the sound of subdued chuckles from the Indians caused us all to turn and look toward them. Their attention was focused on a young puppy that had come from around the edge of the Pueblo building and was trotting across the plaza toward the fire. The puppy's tiny spike tail was wagging back and forth and its floppy ears were half-cocked as if to ask what all the excitement was about. Then, from the darkness beyond the light of the fire, loomed a huge shadowy figure.

"Doenee! Doenee!" called the figure in a deep heavy voice as he came close enough to be seen in the light. Though a horrid looking mask hid his face, I knew from his size that it was the Indian we had seen in the courtyard playing with the puppy. He spotted the puppy next to the fire and began moving with a peculiar rolling gait toward it. The soldiers became silent as they tried to fathom what the appearance of this strange apparition meant. In an instant, my feeling of joy turned to horror as everything seemed to erupt around us.

"They have tricked us!" screamed del Charco hysterically, pulling his sword from its scabbard. "They will kill us all! Attack! Attack before we are lost!"

Campos immediately bound forward. His sword remained sheathed, but his clenched hands were like iron at the end of a giant hammer. He reached the puppy before the Indian, and swept it away with a savage kick from his heavy boot. The puppy gave one short yelp and flew through the air. Its small body struck the side of an *horno* and then slid silently to the ground. The big Indian gave a cry of distress and started moving quickly toward it. He ignored Campos. All his attention was focused on the puppy. As he crossed in front of the fires, Campos stepped forward and his massive fist became a blur as it landed with a dull thud on the Indian's forehead. The force of the blow shattered the mask and sent the Indian backward through the air. He didn't topple over completely, but landed in a sitting position with a dazed look on his face. He shook his head, and tears flowed down his cheeks and a small whimper came from his throat.

The soldiers and Indians started yelling and tried to push forward. With an almost identical and simultaneous motion, Governor de Vargas and Wise Father raised their arms and yelled commands that, through the strength of their wills, kept both sides from rushing toward each other.

Sage was standing beside Wise Father, but she could not be held back. With a quick look at the old man, she slipped below his outstretched arms and bolted toward Lieutenant

Campos and the Indian. The lieutenant stared at the big Indian for a moment, then freed his sword from its scabbard. Holding it high above his head, he planted his feet in preparation for the death stroke. But before he could swing his sword, Sage had sprung upon him. She was on his back with one arm wrapped tightly around his neck. With her other hand she scratched and tore wildly at his face. Wise Father's impassive face became one of alarm and a chorus of yells arose from the Indians. But his hands did not come down. They remained raised in the air, keeping the warriors from rushing Campos.

I heard Carlos draw in a sharp breath beside me when Sage made her leap onto Campos and, ignoring the governor's cries, he ran toward the lieutenant, calling him names that I had never heard him use before. As he ran, he drew the sword I had given him.

"We must fight!" yelled del Charco, leaping after Carlos and loosening his own sword. "The enemy is upon us and the boy is in league with them!" Carlos had almost reached Campos but del Charco was on his heels.

"Carlos! Behind you!" I yelled, running after the two. Carlos' head turned at my cry and he dropped to the ground as del Charco lunged forward with his outstretched sword. Caught off balance, del Charco tripped on Carlos and fell forward to the ground, his sword flying free as he tried to break his fall with outstretched hands. Unarmed, he rose to his feet and moved toward Carlos, who had also gotten up to face del Charco. Carlos held his sword awkwardly in his right hand. It was apparent to me, and to del Charco, that he was unsure of the weapon. Del Charco feinted to Carlos' right, causing Carlos to shift his arm. Immediately del Charco moved back to the left, grabbing Carlos' wrist with his right hand and spinning his whole body so that his left elbow landed solidly in Carlos' mid-section. As Carlos slid to the ground on his hands and knees, trying to suck air back into his empty lungs, del Charco spun his body away, taking Carlos' sword into his hand. I knew in his rage that del Charco was going to kill Carlos. By this time I had reached the two, and I quickly moved between del Charco and Carlos. In his madness, del Charco did not hesitate. He jumped forward and struck toward my right breast. My armor saved my life. The point of the sword hit the metal and deflected off the breastplate, causing me to cry out in pain as the sliding point pierced the flesh of the backside of my right arm above the elbow. To my horror, del Charco continued pushing the blade forward through my arm, only stopping when the hilt of the sword had pressed against my skin.

I reached over with my left hand and grasped his wrist, pulling my body tight against him so that when he tried to remove the sword, he pulled my whole body forward. Carlos, still on his hands and knees, lurched forward and grabbed del Charco around his ankles. He pulled hard and del Charco went down. I screamed again as the sword twisted in my arm, but the blood oozing from the wound had made the hilt slippery and del Charco lost his hold. In a second Carlos and del Charco were a rolling ball of arms and legs fighting a few feet from the fire. I watched them, unable to either move or to look down at the blade in my arm.

"Why don't you help us? Del Charco's trying to kill him!" I heard myself shout at the governor.

"I cannot!" he yelled back. "I must hold the men back! If we try to help all hope of peace is lost! The old Indian knows. See how he keeps his men at bay!"

The governor yelled at del Charco and Campos, ordering

222

them to stop, but they ignored his words. Next to the fire, Campos, his face covered in blood from the many scratches Sage had inflicted, moved in a bizarre dance as he tried to reach behind his shoulders and grab her. He finally caught her at the shoulder and shook her back and forth with his monstrous hand. Yelling wildly, he swung his arm in a vicious downward arc and Sage's body slammed into the ground with a loud thud. She lay unmoving, whether dead or unconscious I could not tell. This was too much for Wise Father. His arms came down and the Indians rushed forward. Governor de Vargas, with a tight grim look on his face, reached down and drew his sword. The signal for attack had been given and the soldiers responded immediately by drawing their weapons. Some took a defensive stance while others hurriedly mounted their horses.

Campos ignored the approaching Indians and focused instead on the giant Indian, who was staring at Sage's body with a shocked look on his face. Taking the hilt of his sword with both hands, Campos again raised his arms high as he readied for a great slashing blow that would split the big Indian's head open. Then, before he could swing his weapon, a high-pitched scream tore through the blackness of the night above him. The loud cry caused Campos to start and he looked at the sky. That brief moment of hesitation proved to be his undoing. The scream came again, followed immediately by the appearance of a huge owl in the darkness above the fires. With wings spread wide and outstretched talons, it tore at Campos' face, driving him back and causing him to drop his sword. The owl's wings slammed against Campos' head and its curved beak slashed at his cheeks and brow. He threw his hands up and swung at the owl, finally catching it backhanded with one fist.

The blow sent the bird spinning into the fire, causing the

223

flames to erupt in a giant shower of orange and yellow sparks. The owl's scream again pierced the night and the shower of sparks grew ever higher as its great flapping wings crashed against the burning wood. Suddenly it burst from the inferno, flying straight up into the nighttime sky. A white flame ringed its feathers and radiated a light of such intensity that the horses reared back with eyes wide and nostrils flared. Campos stood in front of the fire, blood streaming from his face, as the burning owl ascended above him and disappeared in an explosion of blue and red light.

The Indians had stopped their advance at the appearance of the great bird, and then stepped back quickly as it began its fiery climb into the sky. Only the big Indian paid no attention, instead looking from Sage's crumpled body to Campos and back to Sage.

Then he was moving faster than I had ever seen a man move before. Campos saw him coming and turned to meet him, but it was too late. With one hand the Indian grabbed Campos' collar, with the other the back of his belt. In one rapid movement the Indian jerked Campos off his feet and raised him high above his head. With his hands still holding tightly to Campos' clothing, he brought his body crashing toward the ground. At the last second, the Indian shifted so his bent knee, supported by his foot on the ground, was directly beneath Campos. The tearing sound of cracking bones and ripping tendons filled the air as Campos' back splintered like dry wood across the Indian's leg. Campos gave a horrible scream and was silent.

All was quiet except for the panting and scuffling noises coming from Carlos and del Charco as they continued to struggle on the ground. Del Charco was trying to pull himself away from

Carlos and grab his sword in the dirt a few feet away. Carlos, knowing he would be dead if the captain reached his sword, gripped del Charco's collar and pummeled his head. Finally, with a savage blow that split the skin open on Carlos' nose, del Charco freed himself and rolled to his feet in a crouch next to the sword. As he took hold of the hilt, a heavy boot came down on the blade and del Charco was brought up short by the point of the governor's sword pressed against his neck.

"One more move, Captain," the governor hissed through clenched teeth, "and I promise by all that is holy it will surely be your last." Del Charco stared at the governor, and the fire in his eyes was slowly replaced by the dull look of defeat. His fingers gradually opened and he released his hold on the sword.

"Lieutenant Montoya," the governor continued, moving quickly to my side as I started to topple, "place Captain del Charco, and Lieutenant Campos, if he is still alive, under arrest for disobeying the direct orders of their commander." The Governor, with one gentle pull, slid the sword out of my arm and quickly wrapped the torn cloth of my sleeve around the wound.

Carlos had risen slowly to his feet, and, panting from the exertion of his struggle, staggered toward Sage, and then stopped and looked toward me. "The governor's taking care of me. Go to her," I said. He nodded and moved to join Wise Father as he stood over Sage. The other Indians had pushed back against the walls of the building, still stunned by the appearance of the owl and the unexpected fight between del Charco and Carlos.

Together the governor and I stepped over to Carlos, staring over his shoulder at Sage. The big Indian had rolled her onto her back and was gently petting her cheek and making soft unintelligible grunts. The side of Sage's face was swelling and had taken on a mottled purple color. But she was breathing, and as we watched, her eyes opened.

"I'm back, Carlos," she said in a dry voice, looking into her brother's worried eyes. Then she reached up and gently patted the Indian's hand. "Don't worry, Stone. I'll be all right."

"I am as confused as you are, Carlos," Sage said, trying to explain her life in the Indian Pueblo. "Probably more confused. I have known the people of my village all my life, just as I know you and the life we have lived together. The memories of the village are as strong as the memories of you and mommy and the trailer park. To you, life here is something you fell into from our other time. To me, they are the same." Sage struggled with the words, trying to explain how she could be of two worlds. Carlos listened and thought hard about what she said, but I could see many unanswered questions spinning through his head.

I sat with Carlos and Sage discussing the strange events of the night before. We had moved a few hundred yards south from the plaza to a grassy spot beneath the trees on the bank of the river. The weather had changed during the night and it was a chilly blustery morning that held the threat of rain, or even the first snow of the season. My fingers were feeling stiff as I worked with a thick needle and heavy thread to repair the buckle attachment on Carlos' leather scabbard. It had been torn almost completely off during his struggle with del Charco, but was easily fixed. My arm hurt, but as horrendous as it had looked, the damage was not extensive. Fortunately the blade had slid through the skin and only scratched the muscle beneath it before exiting on the other side.

While I sewed the scabbard, they told each other of the things that had passed since the big rainstorm at the home of the man named Doctor Lopez.

I looked up briefly and cringed at the sight of Sage's face. Her eye was swollen almost shut and her cheek was discolored with a massive ugly purple and yellow bruise. I had watched while an Indian woman bathed her wounds after we carried her back into the pueblo. The bruises on her body, now hidden beneath a heavy shawl, had caused great concern among her people, but it appeared that no bones were broken. Carlos had a bright red slash across his nose where del Charco's blow had landed. It looked as if it would scab over in a day or two.

"But if both worlds are the same to you, then which one is the real one?" Carlos asked in a perplexed voice.

Sage let her breath out slowly in a sigh of exasperation. "That is just it, they are both real to me. As to which one I want to stay in, I do not think it is my decision. Whatever caused us to be here, will ultimately decide where I stay. If I am never taken back to the other place, then I will live here at peace with myself. I know now that it is not the same for you, but whether you are here or there, I think, is also beyond your power to decide."

Carlos pressed Sage for more information about her Pueblo life, as if trying to find nuggets of information that would prove she really belonged in the other place and time. Sage seemed hesitant to answer, especially when it came to the more ceremonial aspects of being a Pueblo child. I began to realize that my presence was the cause of her hesitancy. I knew, because of the persecution brought by the Spanish Crown, that many of their religious and cultural habits had been kept hidden from all but members of their village. She was uncomfortable describing in front of me the inner foundations that formed this strange and different culture. I decided it was best that they spend some time by themselves.

"Here," I said to Carlos, handing him his scabbard and belt. "I used a double stitch that will not tear so easily if you should decide to wrestle on the ground again."

After studying my work in appreciative silence, he picked up his sword and frowned when he saw my dried blood on the hilt and metal.

"Do you want me to clean it for you?" I asked.

Carlos shook his head. "You've already done enough for me, Sofía," he said, sheathing his sword. "I don't know if I could have made it without you." He looked up from the sword and our eyes met. "I know now that you have always been there for me, even when I was a little brat not wanting to go to sleep at night. I wish I could remember those times. I wish I could remember the grief I've given you over the years, but I can't. And that makes me sad. Sage has whole memories of her life here, while I have none. I hope your memories are happy ones."

"They are, Carlos," I said softly. "When our families were lost in the revolt, a big hole was left inside me. I had only you, and, because of you, I found a reason to wake each morning and continue on. I hope you are here forever, Carlos. My life would be very empty without you."

We sat silently for a few minutes. Then I stood up.

"Lieutenant Montoya has some saddles he wants me to look at," I said, making up a small fib so I could leave them by themselves. "Maybe by the time I finish, you will have figured everything out."

Carlos and his sister also stood. Carlos looked into my eyes, and took me in his arms, being careful not to brush against my wound, and held me tight. I put my arms around him and buried my face in his shoulder. Then, deep inside, I knew that he and Sage would go. My legs grew weak and my body trembled. For a moment I felt a dull pain in my chest and thought I would faint. Carlos' arms tightened around me.

"Oh, Sofía," he said. "You've captured a part of my heart and that will never change—not in a year, not in three hundred years. Even when, or if, I get back to my own time, you will still have a piece of me." I nodded my head, knowing that if I tried to speak my words would turn to sobs. After a few seconds he released me and reached into his pocket, drawing out a small ribbon woven from thin multi-colored strands of cotton fiber.

"I made this for you this morning from some threads Wise Father gave me," he said. "It is a Celtic ribbon, or at least my best attempt at making one."

"Celtic ribbon? What is that?"

"It is something I saw in a painting just as this whole... adventure...began. It is a link, a link that binds over time and distance between two that love each other. I love you, Sofía, and I don't mean just the love between a brother and sister."

"I know what you mean, you silly goose. I have felt the same way also, and for a longer time than you will ever know," I said, still struggling to keep my voice from breaking. It was too hard, too uncomfortable. I knew I would be crying uncontrollably soon, but I wanted that to be away in a place by myself.

Carlos nodded and Sage gave me a smile.

"You know, you're the best," Carlos said softly.

"That's right, and don't you forget it," I said.

"I'll never forget it, Sofía," he said, ignoring my half-hearted attempt at humor.

"Thank you for taking care of my brother," Sage said. "It was you that brought him back to me." She came forward and hugged me.

"I must go. Lieutenant Montoya has probably sent a search party to find me by now," I mumbled. Sage released her hold and stepped back. I stared at Carlos again, and he moved forward to kiss me on the cheek. At the last second, I turned my head and, for a moment, our lips touched. His eyes opened wide in pleasant surprise. Before he could speak, I pulled away and walked back toward the Palace of the Governors.

Wise Father was standing at the edge of the plaza, gazing over my shoulder toward the river where Carlos and Sage stood. He held the puppy Campos had kicked the night before and was gently stroking its head. I stopped next to him and scratched the puppy under its chin. Its tail gave a small wag, and a small pink tongue tried to lick at my hand. I turned, and together Wise Father and I watched Carlos and Sage walk up the path alongside the river. Their heads were bent close to each other and they were deep in conversation. Then, as if feeling our eyes upon them, they stopped and looked back. Sage said something to Carlos and came over to us.

"I'm going for a walk with my Dream Brother," she said, giving the old man a hug, and then pausing to scratch the puppy's back. "Tell Deer Dancer that I'll keep my blanket wrapped around me so I won't catch a cold." Wise Father nodded without speaking and returned her hug. Walking stiffly she rejoined her brother. A moment later they disappeared around a curve in the path.

"Things are as they should be," the old man said in his halting Spanish. His eyes grew moist and I tried to swallow the lump in my throat.

15

The Path Home

Sage and I walked up the trail until we had traveled far into the foothills of the Sangre de Cristo Mountains. At times we would speak, but mostly we moved forward in silence, each thinking our own thoughts.

The clouds hung heavy and dark above us, and after a while a drizzle of rain mixed with specks of snow began to fall. Within a few minutes it had turned into a steady rain. We moved under the shelter of a huge pine tree and sat next to each other with our knees drawn up under our chins.

Sage pulled her shawl over our heads, providing some shelter from the rain. But soon our impromptu tent was saturated and the water dropping onto it made wet splashing sounds. A particularly big black cloud passed slowly over our tree and the rain fell harder. There was no lightening or thunder, just the steady plop-plop of water striking the shawl and the drizzling noise of the rain landing on the trees and undergrowth around us.

"Are you cold?" I asked. Sage shook her head.

"Do you think we should start walking back?"

"Let us wait until it has passed," she answered, pulling the shawl further down over our heads to shelter our knees and lower legs. The thick cloud cover coupled with the wet shawl made it seem as though it was nighttime. Together we sat quietly on the wet pine needles in the mountain forest. As the minutes passed, the cocoon we had built around us grew warmer and I had to fight to stay awake. Beside me I heard Sage's steady breath and knew she was asleep. I yawned a few more times and let my eyes close. The last thing I remember was my head slipping forward until my chin came to rest against my chest.

We were awakened by a voice calling our names. I don't think either of us knew how long we had slept, maybe a few minutes or maybe for hours. The grass and pine needles were gone and beneath us was a smooth wet floor.

I reached out my hand and pushed the shawl away from our faces. It was soaking wet, and its rough course weave had been replaced by velvety softness. Abruptly the darkness beyond the cloth disappeared and there was a bright light coming in through the thin crack where the fabric and the floor came together.

"Carlos. Sage. Are you in there somewhere?" the voice asked.

We heard some shuffling sounds and the heavy wetness of the velvet rubbed against our heads and backs as the cloth was pulled off us. With a sudden jerk it was gone and we squinted in the bright light of crystal chandeliers. Standing in front of us, with the drapes from the window bunched together in his hands, was Doctor Lopez wearing his green raincoat.

We rose to our feet slowly, looking in stunned silence at the scene around us. A shallow pool of water littered with twigs, leaves and shattered glass covered the floor. The window frame hung bent and torn on its hinges. The light in the room spilled out beyond the twisted window, illuminating the tiny droplets that fell gently from the sky. Off in the distance there was an occasional flash of lightning, followed a few seconds later by the muted rumble of thunder.

The holly bush Doctor Lopez had sculpted into an owl was a mass of scorched and burned branches. Small wisps of smoke rose from it. As we watched, the last glowing embers that were its eyes died with a soft sizzling whisper.

"What...what happened, Doctor Lopez?" I asked, my voice shaking.

"I thought you could tell me," the Doctor said. I didn't answer. Where would any answer start? Sage just looked at the doctor with wide eyes. "One minute I was trying to grab the ladder," he continued, "and then a second later I was rolling in the grass. It looks like lightning struck the bush and blew everything around it away—including me. After it hit, I came looking for you two, but the power was cut off and I couldn't find you under the drapes."

He studied us carefully for a moment. "Are you all right?" he asked.

"I think so," I said.

"My head hurts," Sage said, "but otherwise I'm okay."

Doctor Lopez reached out and gently touched Sage's cheek. "You must have hit your face. You're going to have quite a shiner there. And you," he said turning back to me," are bleeding from a cut on your nose. It looks like a piece of flying glass nicked you."

I raised my hand, touching the blood slowly rolling down my nose. Doctor Lopez's hand went under his rubber coat, and reappeared a moment later with a clean white handkerchief.

"Let's see if we can get it to stop bleeding. I don't think you need stitches, but we can't send you home looking like this." He stepped forward and dabbed at my cut nose with his handkerchief. "Thank goodness nobody was badly hurt, although my poor owl certainly looks a little smoke damaged."

My brow furrowed at the mention of the owl.

"It wasn't the lightning that burned up the owl. It was the fire in front of the pueblo," I blurted out.

Doctor Lopez appeared not to have heard and continued dabbing at my nose with the handkerchief.

"We were back in Santa Fe with de Vargas and everything would have been a horrible mess except for the owl and the way he attacked Lieutenant Campos when he tried to kill the big Indian after he threw Sage onto the ground, and then the way he flew out of the fire when everybody was getting ready to fight because their arms had come down and...," I broke off in mid-sentence. Even to myself I sounded like a babbling fool.

Doctor Lopez finished wiping my wound, looking steadily at me from behind his silver framed spectacles. "De Vargas? If memory serves me right, we were talking about him before the storm struck," he said.

"It was just like you said," Sage broke in nodding rapidly. "Only it wasn't. He came offering religious tolerance and the peaceful reconquest was happening like you described, but then everything was different."

Doctor Lopez turned his gaze to her and she became silent. Sage didn't look away, but instead stared steadily into his eyes. Finally, he gave an almost imperceptible nod of his head.

"You already know," she said softly. "You know everything that happened to us."

Doctor Lopez smiled. "I know historical records of that time describe a message of peace that led to a bloodless reconquest and an Indian culture that continues to this day," he said.

A puzzled expression crossed her face. "That's true, but it isn't the whole story."

"Not by a long shot," I said. "If Sage hadn't tried to stop Lieutenant Campos, and the owl hadn't appeared..."

"Or if Carlos hadn't kept Captain del Charco from helping Campos, or if de Vargas hadn't had a woman, named Sofía, disguised as a soldier in his company, there would have been a horrible battle," Sage interrupted. She paused and then pressed on. "Did you know about all this?" she asked Doctor Lopez.

"There are many things missing from the story of the reconquest," he said, carefully choosing his words. "I'm afraid the journals kept by Governor de Vargas make no mention of an owl or a woman soldier."

"But that is the way it happened. I saw it. I was part of the village, a village I had known all my life. How could that be?" Sage asked. "And how was it that I have a life in

235

the village that I knew, while Carlos didn't know anything of his life there, though everybody else did? Are we both crazy, Doctor Lopez?" A sense of frustration filled her voice and she was close to tears. The doctor reached out and placed his hands on her shoulders.

"No, Sage," he said, "I don't think you are at all crazy. This is a strange world we live in, and there are not always answers to our questions. Sometimes, all we can do is continue to search for those answers realizing that though they may come in time, they may also never come at all. I have seen many unusual things in the course of my life as an antiquarian, and I have learned to live with the questions that arise from my studies. You and Carlos have a long life ahead, and I wouldn't be at all surprised if the answers you seek are on the path ahead of you."

I considered Doctor Lopez's words. Still, one of the questions asked by Sage continued to nag at me. "There is something else bothering me, Doctor Lopez, but before I ask you about it, I want you to answer Sage's question. Did you know where that bolt of lightning sent us?" I asked.

"Eh? Well...when that lightning hit I was holding onto the gutter for dear life, and then I was flying through the air. I can't really say much more than that."

"Can't say, or won't say?" I pressed. The doctor gave me an appreciative smile, as if pleased by my quick response.

"I'll tell you what. Why don't you ask about whatever's bothering you, while I decide how to answer your first question."

I hesitated, studying the doctor with a calculating eye, and then shrugged my shoulders in resignation. "Before we left, that is, before the storm hit, you told us how Governor de

Vargas reconquered the Pueblo Indians peacefully by letting them live in the way that they were accustomed to."

"Yes, that is what I told you."

"From the way you described it," I continued, "I thought the governor was one of the good guys. But several times he talked about using force against the Indians and how he would have no choice but to attack the Pueblo. He was prepared to do that, even if it meant killing a lot of people. Is he remembered as a good guy because everything broke his way at the end?"

Doctor Lopez considered the question. "I think," he said, "that he was neither a good or bad guy. He was a military commander during a time and in a place where using violent and naked force was to be expected. In fact, for many years following the reconquest, there were still many Indians that refused to accept Spanish rule and continued to rebel against de Vargas and his soldiers. Against those, de Vargas used the power of his command to quell the uprisings, as did other governors in later years. Many Indians and a smaller number of Spaniards died in those rebellions. Looking back we know that though subsequent battles were violently fought and brutally won by de Vargas, he largely kept his promise and did not interfere in the Indian's way of life. This is much different than what was occurring in other parts of the country where the defeated Indian tribes lost everything—including, in many instances, their homes, their land and their lives. The Pueblo Indians, however, kept the homes they had occupied centuries before the arrival of the first Spaniards. That's why today the Pueblos practice their religion in a way and place that is theirs.

"And that is why the Spaniards and Pueblo Indians became friends and allies. As I told you earlier, before the storm, the tolerance the Spaniards offered to the Pueblos after the revolt is something very rare in mankind's development. But it provides an excellent opportunity, three hundred years later, to learn how mutual respect and tolerance enables a peaceful co-existence that could never be achieved through force of arms."

The muffled electronic pulse of a ringing phone interrupted Doctor Lopez. He reached beneath his raincoat and came out with his cell phone. He looked at the buttons over the top of his glasses for a moment before pressing one. The ringing stopped and he lifted it to his ear.

"Hello," he said, and then listened to the crackle of the voice at the other end. Mom, I thought

"No, we haven't finished. Things are still a bit messy here. Lightning and rain from that last thunder storm set us back a bit." He paused as the voice on the other end of the line spoke.

"Everybody is fine, but Carlos and Sage got a bit bruised from a bolt of lightning that struck a little too close for comfort." The crackle on the phone became faster and louder.

"No, no, they're fine. I can bring them home now. We can finish cleaning up tomorrow." He paused to listen. "Are you sure? I don't mind driving them over." Another pause as the voice on the other end crackled again. Doctor Lopez hesitated a moment before speaking. "Okay, if you're sure it doesn't put you out."

The voice at the other end of the line said something and the doctor gave a small nod as if the person he was talking to could see him.

"Then we'll see you in about five minutes. Good-bye."

 238

Doctor Lopez replaced the phone in the pocket hidden beneath the raincoat and looked up at us. "That was your mother. She got off work early and is on her way over to pick you up."

That kind of blew my mind. As far as Mom knew, we had been at Doctor Lopez's for only a few hours. But it had actually been almost two months since Sage and I had last seen her. For some reason, the everyday worries of homework assignments and soccer shoes seemed pretty pale in comparison to what we had encountered.

Sage's thoughts, however, were on the Indians of the village.

"Doctor Lopez," she asked softly, "when de Vargas used his soldiers against the Pueblos in later years, were they fighting against the Indians who were in Santa Fe during the reconquest?"

The doctor hesitated before answering. "According to Spanish documents from that time—the Indians didn't record what happened—de Vargas returned to El Paso and came back with hundreds of settlers. When they reached Santa Fe, the Pueblo Indians living in the Palace of the Governors had had a change of heart and refused to leave. That is when de Vargas used force to retake the capital."

Sage looked down at her hands and spoke in an almost inaudible whisper. "Were many of the Indians killed?"

Doctor Lopez didn't respond, and Sage looked up and saw her answer in his solemn eyes. Tears began rolling down her cheeks and she began to weep silently. The doctor moved forward and she buried her face in his chest as he wrapped his arms tightly around her. Sage's body shook with each breath. I stood awkwardly for a few seconds before reaching out and placing my hand softly on her shoulder.

"I wouldn't worry too much," I said, trying to reassure her, "Governor de Vargas liked Wise Father, and he certainly wouldn't do anything against Stone."

"Oh, Carlos," she said in a voice muffled by Doctor Lopez's raincoat, "you saw how it was. Once the fighting begins, no one is safe. And even if Wise Father and Stone were unharmed, how about all the others that were part of my village? Can you tell me that they would be all right?"

I thought back to the soldiers drawing their swords and the Indians rushing toward the soldiers before the owl appeared. I remained silent. After several minutes the sobs wracking Sage's body slowed and Doctor Lopez pushed her gently away so he could look into her tear-stained face.

"Sage," he said firmly, "we don't know which Indians died. The only history we have is from what the Spaniards wrote and it is silent on the names of those who fell in battle. But we can take comfort in the knowledge that what transpired during the days of the reconquest allowed the Pueblo Indians to keep their way of life into this time three hundred years later. I know it doesn't help ease the pain you feel, but the understanding that came from the events of that night in Santa Fe saved the Pueblo Indian culture while teaching a lesson of tolerance that, we can only hope, is not lost on the world around us today."

Sage tried to muster a smile, but it was a sad one and tears continued to run from her eyes. She brushed them away with her blouse sleeve and again looked at the disarray that surrounded them.

"This place is a mess," she said in a thick voice. "We came here to help clean it up, and it's worse than ever."

Doctor Lopez gave a laugh. "Never mind about the

240

room. You've both been through a lot tonight," he said. The doctor looked out the window as Mom's headlights appeared at entrance to his driveway.

"Your mother is here and the storm looks like it is gone for the night. We can cleanup tomorrow, and perhaps, if you feel up to it, discuss your questions further."

Sage nodded silently and released her grasp on the doctor.

"But before you leave," Doctor Lopez said, moving to a wooden chest next to the wall, "I want to give you something from my collection. After the events of tonight, you both deserve a keepsake to remind you, as if you need reminding, of what has passed."

He opened the chest and took out a small box. He handed it to Sage. Then the doctor reached back inside and came out with a long, heavy paper swathed bundle. He handed it to me.

Sage opened the box and gasped as she gently removed a *Katchina* doll. A brittle rabbit-skin skirt was wrapped around its body, and small feathers curling with age crowned the head. It looked like the one she told me Wise Father had been making when she first dreamed of me on my horse. Sage took a deep breath as memories of an old Indian carefully fitting each feather came rushing to her.

My package was heavy. I carefully pulled the paper away and stared at a cracked leather belt with a scabbard and sword. On the tarnished hilt were dark dried flecks. I ran my fingernail along the metal and watched as a flake came loose and fluttered to the floor.

"It looks like dried blood," Doctor Lopez said, "blood that should have been wiped clean years ago."

I nodded and stared at the metal buckle still firmly sewn to the leather with a heavy double stitch. Turning the belt over in my hands, I looked for the etching on the backside. A small carving of a tree could be faintly seen in the cracks in the leather. I felt a dull pain in my chest. I think, if I had been alone, I would have cried out her name.

From outside came the beep of Mom's horn.

"It's time to go," Doctor Lopez said, "I'll walk you out."

The three of us moved together in silence through the Great Room, down the entry hall and out the front door. Mom had gotten out of the car and was walking over to the burned remnants of the bush in front of the battered window. I looked over at Sage and she smiled. We both took off, jumping from the porch and running toward her. She looked at us in surprise when we wrapped our arms around her.

"My goodness," she said in a flustered voice, "You'd think you haven't seen me in a year."

"More like three hundred years," I said.

"How about over three hundred years?" Sage said.

Mom gave us a puzzled look that quickly turned to concern when she saw, in the light spilling from the window of the room, Sage's bruised face and my cut nose.

"*Dios mio*, what happened to you?" she asked.

"Lightning hit the bush and Carlos and I were standing in front of the window," Sage said. "It threw us...uh, it tossed us across the room. Carlos got a cut on his nose and I banged my cheek, but otherwise we're okay."

"Hmmm, well that's more than can be said for the bush," Mom said, looking over at the charred branches.

Doctor Lopez joined us and greeted her, all the while apologizing for our cuts and bruises.

"Don't worry about it, Doctor," she said. "That comes with having kids. Although, I must admit, I never expected to be patching wounds from a lightning bolt. I'm sorry about your owl. You put a lot of work into it, and now its nothing but burnt leaves and branches."

"I guess I'll just have to make another," the doctor said in a matter-of-fact voice.

Mom nodded, giving him a strange look. Finally she looked at her watch and gave a start. "C'mon kids, it is getting late. Say goodnight to the doctor so we can get going."

After the last good-byes had been said, we walked over to the car, leaving Doctor Lopez standing by the bush. With a final wave we climbed in the car, backed down the driveway, and turned into the street.

Sage and I watched through the back window as Doctor Lopez stared after us. As we moved down the street, the clouds broke for a moment and he was bathed in moonlight. Doctor Lopez slowly turned, looking at a large spruce tree growing at the edge of the garden.

An owl, with wings spread wide, flew from the tree. It circled once over the doctor's head and then disappeared above the trees.